BULLET PROOF

LOVE UNDERCOVER, BOOK 4

L.K. SHAW

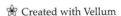 Created with Vellum

CHAPTER 1

Seven months ago

ADRENALINE PUMPED THROUGH MY VEINS. I felt invincible. As though nothing could touch me. It was always like this right before a big bust.

The thrill.

The rush.

I lived for it. I loved taking down drug dealers. Even more so after the cartel killed my eldest brother. My other brother, Manuel, said I was addicted to it. Like my own personal drug. Just as deadly as something bought off the street. Because when a cop feels he's untouchable, he makes mistakes.

Gun securely held between my hands, its muzzle pointed toward the ground, I waited impatiently for the signal. The cold from the metal wall of the warehouse seeped through my uniform. Despite the nip of winter in the air, it felt good against the heat of my rapidly flowing blood. My feet twitched with the need to move.

I was antsy and ready for some action.

In perfect defense formation, my gaze homed in on the man in front of me while I waited for my cue to follow behind him. The tension radiating off him and the man at my back told me it was coming.

The unit leader's fist pounded on the warehouse door. "Chicago PD. Open up."

There it was. We breached the door, and the shuffling sound of fifteen pairs of feet was loud in the quiet night. I scuttled in, panning the interior with eyes and pistol, searching for the two men we'd confirmed were inside. We fanned out, slowly moving forward, everyone on high alert.

"Drop your weapon," a voice yelled from my two o'clock.

Gunfire erupted at the same time I spotted a suspect holding the semi-automatic, and I dove behind a pallet stacked with wooden crates. Splinters ricocheted off it, and I flinched, my ears ringing.

My gaze darted around, taking in my team's position. A quick peek over the top of the pallet confirmed the shooter's location. *Where was the other guy?* I ducked back down.

"Cover me," I yelled to Garrison, the teammate nearest me.

He nodded, and like a jack-in-the-box, sprung up and started laying down fire while I dashed across the open space. I needed to get closer to the men trying to take us out. I slid behind another pallet at the same time the second gunman came into sight. There was a lull in the exchange of fire.

"You're surrounded. Put down your weapons and come out with your hands up."

They responded with a new round of gunfire. I jackknifed up, and my gun spit bullets. A cry of pain followed, and several shouts from the other assailant came right on its tail. Taking the opportunity, I was once again on the move. Three, maybe four feet, from my next spot of protection more gunfire came. I stumbled and crashed to the floor, rolling behind a shelf stacked with more wooden boxes.

A burning sensation spread through my thigh that quickly transformed into a pain unlike anything I'd felt before. I shifted, and black spots danced in my vision. My fingers clutched my leg. The pain turned to an aching throb that radiated through my entire body. Pulling my hand away, my gloved fingertips glistened with wetness. A glance down was all the confirmation I needed. Blood pooled under my leg.

"Rodriguez, Code Thirty," I said into the walkie clipped to my shoulder.

"Fuck," came the immediate response.

Shuffling sounds echoed through the warehouse's high ceilings.

"Down! Get down on the ground!" came on its heels.

I sat there, pressed against the crate at my back, trying to put pressure on my leg, but fuck, it was agony. A noise to my left had me jerking my gun in that direction, but I quickly lowered it.

"Shit, Pablo. Where are you hit?" Oliver Garrison asked, tucking his Glock back in its holster.

"Left thigh. I think my leg's broke too." I wiped the sweat off my brow. "Call Vicky."

"What?"

Oliver moved my leg, and a groan rumbled through my chest. "I need you to call Victor. He's in a car down the road waiting with Brody. Let him know what's going on."

While my buddy followed my request, another teammate came and took over.

"You doing okay? Not hit anywhere else, are you?" Peterman asked.

I shook my head. "I don't think so."

"You should have waited," he said.

"Excuse me?"

"I saw you move forward right before you got hit. You didn't even wait for someone to cover you."

My head jerked at the accusation in his tone.

"Ambulance is on its way. Victor's going to head to the hospital," Oliver interrupted.

Peterman glanced over at him. "You got this?"

Garrison nodded. The other man stood and walked away without another word.

"What a dick."

I turned my head toward my friend, but he was glaring at the retreating man. I replayed the entire scene. I was sure I'd hit one of the gunmen before moving into my new position. Granted, the second suspect hadn't been in sight, but I'd heard him. He'd been more concerned about his friend, which was why I'd gone ahead and tried to get closer.

Had I gotten too cocky?

I OPENED my eyes and blinked against the bright artificial lighting above my head. Beeping sounds pierced my eardrums. Pain registered next. I turned my head, and the first person I spotted was Ines. Her eyes were closed, her cheeks tear-stained. Next to her, his expression more grim than usual, was Brody. He was staring straight ahead, but then he blinked and his eyes met mine. I managed a pain-filled half smile.

He didn't even move, but like she was that attuned to him, Ines shifted, and her eyes opened. Her gaze landed on me, and with a cry, she dashed over.

"Oh my god, Pablo," she choked out my name and clutched my hand, bringing her lips down to meet my knuckles.

"I'm okay."

Brody rose and stood at my sister's side comforting her. "You in pain?"

I grimaced. "A little."

He nodded, squeezed Ines's waist, whispered in her ear, and headed out the door.

"You had us so worried," Ines said.

I turned my head back toward her.

"Papa, Manny, and Vicky have been here waiting for you to wake up. They wouldn't let us all stay in your room at once, but they're in the family room down the hall."

Of course they were. I'd expect nothing less from my family. "I'm fine. What's a little bullet wound?" I joked.

"Don't forget the broken leg," Brody piped up from the doorway. I hadn't heard him return. "Nurse will be in in a second."

I nodded my thanks. "Figured the leg was broken."

"They took you in for surgery as soon as you arrived," Ines added.

"What time is it?"

"Around four," Brody said.

"Shit, why aren't you guys home in bed?" I asked.

My sister gave me a look that said if I hadn't been stuck in this hospital bed with a bullet wound she'd smack me. "Don't be dense. Of course we were going to be here. You're our brother. And you were shot, you idiot."

"Thanks, I'd forgotten," I drawled.

"Ines," Brody warned when she opened her mouth, no doubt to lay into me, broken leg be damned. She snapped it shut.

"We should probably all get some sleep," he added.

The door opened, and a nurse stepped in. "Good morning, Mr. Rodriguez. Nice to see you awake. What's your pain level on a scale of one to ten?"

"I don't know. Maybe a four."

"Just press this button, and a dose of pain meds will be administered through your IV."

"Thanks." I pressed the button she'd indicated and then sank back into the hospital bed waiting for relief to kick in.

"I'll be back to check on you in a little while," she said before disappearing out the door as quickly as she'd arrived.

Despite only being awake for a few minutes, my lids grew heavy.

"Now that Ines has seen for herself that you're doing okay, why don't we let you get some rest," Brody said, for which I was grateful.

From her hesitation, Ines wasn't ready to go, but he

laid a hand on her shoulder. She reached up and squeezed it, with a nod. Then she leaned down and brushed a kiss over my cheek, the scent of her familiar perfume comforting me.

"Te amo, hermano," she whispered.

"Yo también te quiero."

"We'll let everyone know you're doing okay, and we'll stop by later this morning after you've had time to rest." She tugged on one of my curls like she had when we were kids.

I sent her a sleepy smile. "Thanks for being here when I woke up."

"Of course."

The two of them left, and my eyes drifted shut. I was floating in the state that hovered just on the edge of sleep when the crack of gunfire shattered the quiet in my mind.

CHAPTER 2

Present day

MAISIE LOOKED MORE and more like her father every day. Although calling Henry Warren Caldwell III, a father was a joke. He was nothing more than a sperm donor. Regardless, the older my daughter got, the more she resembled him. They both had the same blue eyes. A bright blue, like the kind you'd find in the sky on a cloudless day. Her nose was patrician, just like his. And she had that perfect cupid's bow shaped lips. I'd been a starry-eyed, stupid teenage girl over those lips.

The only thing my daughter seemed to have gotten from me was my wavy, unimaginative, plain brown hair. There wasn't anything special about it. I couldn't boast natural highlights. Nope, Maisie was stuck with my regular old mud brown hair. Otherwise, she was all her father. In looks only anyway. She didn't get his personality, thank god.

"Mama, don't forget my floaties," she piped up, shaking me out of my thoughts.

"I have them right here, don't worry." To prove my point, I tugged them out of my giant bag that doubled as a purse.

My daughter bounced excitedly up and down, antsy for the lap swimming to be over and the open swimming to begin. I managed to wrangle her arms into the inflatable rings. The faces of a blonde girl with a long braid wearing a powder blue dress and a snowman with a carrot nose and giant buck teeth stared up at me from them. Hand-in-hand, we stepped out of the women's locker room and entered the humid pool area. The scent of chlorine was overpowering and nearly burned my eyes.

Several other mothers with children milled around as well as a group of teenage boys, all anxious to get in the pool. I only hoped the teens stayed in the deep end, because they tended to get rowdy, splashing each other, and cannonballing off the diving board.

I glanced toward the lone figure swimming down the second from the outside lane, his powerful strokes moving his body fluidly through the water. My eyes stayed locked on him while he finished his final lap.

"Mama," Maisie whined.

I gently squeezed her hand.

"We have to wait, honey," I mumbled back, unable to look away. He reached the edge of the pool, and with muscled arms, the kind that was my kryptonite, hauled himself up and out of it. Water cascaded off his body, and every bit of saliva dried up in my mouth while I took him in.

He was everything I could have imagined. Only better.

Those shoulders. Oh, fuck, those washboard abs. Wet swim trunks stuck to his skin outlining what appeared to be a pretty impressive package. I barely refrained from moaning. My gaze reluctantly moved to his muscular thighs, focusing on the scar on the left one. It was the only flaw I could see. I studied it a second longer. *Was that from a gunshot wound?*

A swim cap covered his head and goggles blocked the sight of his eyes so the only discernible features I could make out were his hawk-like nose and full lips, the bottom one slightly bigger than the top. Something about him seemed familiar, but I couldn't quite figure out what.

I followed the trail of one particular droplet of water. It ran down his neck and continued on a path along his sculpted chest that reminded me of one of those Greek god statues at the museum.

"Mama, come on." There was a sharp tug on my hand.

My gaze darted away from the sexy specimen and down to my daughter who continued trying to drag me to the other end of the pool.

"We can't go in yet, sweetie. Remember, we have to wait until they remove the lane ropes. You have to be patient."

Telling an almost four-year old to be patient was like asking a bird not to fly. Or a flower not to bloom. My daughter especially. I guess that was one more thing she got from her sperm donor.

"Michele?"

A shiver darted across my neck, and goosebumps puckered across my flesh at the voice. It was a deep bass. The kind that rumbled through my chest and gave me a cold chill. I slowly pivoted a half-turn.

In front of me, still dripping wet, but no longer wearing his swim cap or goggles, stood Pablo Rodriguez. His honey-colored gaze met mine, and another shiver danced across my skin. I couldn't look away even if I tried.

I croaked and cleared my throat before trying again, feeling like an idiot. "Hi."

He was just as gorgeous as the first time I'd seen him. Most of his dark curls were plastered against his head from the cap he'd worn, but several already started to spring back to their unruly tousled mess. My fingers itched to muss it entirely.

"It's nice to see you again. I didn't realize you were a member here." His gaze danced around to indicate the rec center.

"We just moved into the neighborhood and only recently joined." I laid my arm around Maisie's shoulders and pulled her against me, giving her the reassurance she needed when someone new entered our circle.

In a move that surprised me, Pablo knelt, smiling at the little girl at my side. Something about that smile melted my insides into a gooey mess.

"Hello there. You must be Maisie. I'm Pablo. My sister Ines has told me all about you. She said you do a great job holding baby Zoey."

If him introducing himself to my daughter shocked me, it was nothing compared to her response. A giant grin took up her entire face and her eyes sparkled with excitement. My normally reserved-around-strangers daughter beamed. "You know Zoey? Her is my favorite. Is her here? I wanna hold the baby."

Pablo's smile widened even further showing bright

white teeth, and I nearly whimpered. My god, it should be illegal for a man to be that beautiful.

"No, I'm sorry, she's not here right now." He glanced around and then whispered conspiratorially. "Can I let you in on a secret?"

Maisie's eyes widened and she nodded.

"She's my favorite, too."

She chortled, then immediately turned to me and her voice boomed. "Mama, did you hear that?"

I smiled down at her. "Yes, baby, I heard."

My gaze shifted, and those beautiful golden orbs were locked on me. Pablo rose slowly to his feet, his eyes still trained on my face. I couldn't pull away from the intensity I saw in them. The shrill sound of a whistle made me jerk.

"Open swim is now in session," the loud tinny voice boomed through the overhead speaker.

"Mama." Maisie tugged on my arm again, her obsession with Pablo's niece clearly forgotten.

I gestured over my shoulder with a thumb. "Sorry, that's our cue."

Pablo brushed off my words with a smile. "You don't have to apologize. Have fun. It was nice seeing you again."

"Thanks, you as well."

"Bye, Maisie," he said.

She waved with one hand at the same time she pulled me harder with the other. "Bye."

With that, I turned my back on Pablo and let my daughter lead the way to the water, but for the rest of the day, I couldn't get him out of my mind.

CHAPTER 3

Getting shot was a bitch. Recovering from a gunshot wound? Even more so. Trying to minimize my still-present limp, I strode through the station house like I had every day since my return to full duty nearly a month ago.

I glanced around at the place I called my second home. All the desks were in the same spot. The dinner plate sized stain still remained on the carpet just outside the break room. My gaze landed on the familiar "out of order" sign taped to the coffeemaker. A cacophony of voices echoed as loud as always. Everything in here was exactly as it had been before I'd been shot nearly eight months ago.

Except me.

Twelve fucking years. I'd made it twelve years being a cop without ever taking a bullet.

I weaved in and out of loiterers shooting the shit and officers parked at desks taking witness statements and processing releases before finally reaching my own. The ragged chair creaked under my weight, and I let out a relieved sigh to finally be off my feet. Stretching my leg out in front of me, I shifted to get more comfortable and then tried digging into the piles of never-ending paperwork.

My mind wouldn't focus on it though. Instead my thoughts kept drifting back to the encounter I'd had earlier today. Seeing Michele and her daughter at the rec center had been a surprise. Most definitely a pleasant one. It had taken me a moment to recognize her with her dark brown hair pulled up, but then she'd turned her head just enough in my direction. It was definitely her. My initial intent had been to just grab my towel and head to the locker room, but her name left my mouth before I could stop it.

I'd sensed the wariness in Maisie at my approach. I hadn't been sure if it was me specifically or just a general nervousness around a stranger. Either way, I didn't want her afraid. Ines had told me about the little girl's infatuation with my niece, so I'd hoped to put her at ease with the mention of her. Man, that kid's smile was enough to pull even the grumpiest person out of a bad mood.

I would have paid money to see the same smile on her mother's face. Something told me it would have hit me just as hard, but much lower. What was it about her? I'd only met her once before, and we'd hardly spent more than ten minutes in each other's company, but that first glance had me intrigued. Over the last couple years, I'd heard bits and pieces of her story from Ines. Michele had had a rough life, and I'd seen shadows of that pain lingering in her eyes. Those shadows had called out to me.

Not that it mattered. I had to be close to fifteen years her senior. Pushing away that depressing thought, I forced myself to focus on the stacks of reports on my desk that needed my attention. It wasn't long before I was intent on my work.

"You look like shit, Rodriguez." Oliver collapsed into the chair opposite me with a smart-ass grin across his face.

"That's not what your mom said when I left her house this morning," I volleyed back.

He slouched in his seat and kicked his heels up on the corner of my desk, crossing one ankle over the other and threading his fingers over his lap. "Look at you with the lame mom jokes. I'm sorry, how old are we again?"

"Can I help you?" Garrison was the type to easily get off topic if I didn't reign him back in. Good cop, but far too easily distracted.

"Talked to one of my nurse friends down at Rush today. Man, the things that woman can do with her mouth should be outlawed." He made a lewd gesture, and I grimaced.

"Please, stop. Does this have any relation to actual police work?" I griped.

"You're no fun anymore." Oliver gave an aggrieved sigh. "Anyway, it would seem that over the last six months, there's been a rise in deaths related to Fentanyl overdoses. By people who don't have a prescription, I should add. Now that Miguel Álvarez is dead and the Juarez Cartel lost its foothold in the city, the Sinaloa Cartel has slithered its way over here. They're the biggest supplier of that lovely little narcotic."

I glared at him. "Emilio Salazar had been trying to take over the drug trade in Chicago for nearly two years. Now he's got it. That's what started the whole civil war within the Juarez Cartel in the first place. Alejandro González didn't think his uncle was taking the threat seriously enough."

"And now they're both dead," Oliver pointed out.

Good riddance, too. Not only had Álvarez's people killed Ernesto, but Ines had been permanently scarred after taking a knife across her face by his nephew. The world was a better place with the two of them burning in hell.

"I hear the Feds are still salty about losing out on the King bust. Almost eight months later, and they keep whining about it. Speaking of, how's the leg?" he gestured with his chin.

"The doctor cleared me for duty a month ago," I said, trying not to sound defensive.

Oliver's arms mimicked his leg's pose, and he stared me down. "That's not what I asked."

"Don't worry. I've still got your back if we head into another takedown. I know how nervous they make you." The smirk on my face felt forced, but I maintained the expression.

Oliver flipped me the finger. "Speaking of takedowns, Captain has a new task for us. One you're not going to be excited about. Then again, considering you've only been back for a short time, it's probably a good thing."

"What's that supposed to mean?"

He single shoulder shrugged. "There's just been some chatter."

I drew back. *Chatter?* "About?"

He didn't meet my gaze for several seconds. Oliver wasn't normally one to hedge. In fact, he was, more often than not, the first one to start gossiping like a schoolgirl. For him to hesitate? It wasn't good.

"Garrison," I growled after the extended silence became too much.

He blew out a sharp breath of air. "A couple of the guys aren't sure if you're ready to be back. They're worried about you."

My body stiffened. "That's bullshit. What you mean is *they're* not ready for me to be back. No doubt it's Peterman leading the witch hunt."

"Look, forget about him. He's an asshole. Like you said, the doc cleared you."

There was a small part of me that wondered if the guys should be concerned.

"What's this new assignment?" I changed the subject.

His lips turned up in that smile that always made me nervous. "It's not the thrill of danger you're used to—I get that honor this time—but you…are now…my handler," he announced with an idiotic amount of dramatics.

My pulse kicked up a notch, and I breathed through it. "What do you mean your *handler*?"

Under my desk, I cracked each of my knuckles.

"Cap sent me undercover inside Los Lobos, and he wants you to be my point of contact within the department."

Jesus. They were the largest Hispanic gang in Chicago, and they had direct ties to the Sinaloa Cartel. "What's the end game?" I asked.

"Los Lobos and the Spanish Serpents have always been bitter rivals. Now that Salazar has moved his operation into the city, these guys are on the verge of an all-out war, because he and Los Lobos are taking over the Fentanyl trade. Prior to the cartel's arrival, the Serpents were the prime supplier. While gangs aren't specifically our jurisdiction, the product they're trafficking is. I'll be working on bringing down Ricardo Morales."

Shit. "Are we talking about *El Diablo*?"

Oliver nodded, his expression finally turning serious. "One and the same. We're leaving Salazar to the DEA, but Cap has his eyes on Morales and Los Lobos."

"Christ." The breath exploded out of me. "How deep are you?"

"Not very. Yet. They've got me doing petty shit right now. Courier stuff. However, I've been recruited to be part of a robbery planned for tomorrow night. I keep pushing for more involvement, but not trying too hard or too quickly. Cap wanted me to wait on trying to get any deeper until I had you on board."

"And who am I supposed to be?" I needed a cover as well, in case Morales or any other members happened to catch us meeting. Everything had to be discussed in person. No phone calls. No email exchanges. Of course we'd take precautions, but there was always the risk of being seen together.

"You, my friend, are my cousin Ángel on my mother's side. You've recently crossed the border, no papers, to try and make money to send back to your beloved madre in Torreón."

Fantastic. "And when does this new assignment start?"

Oliver pulled his feet off my desk and laid his crossed forearms, chin resting on them, atop the faded wooden surface. His smirk made me twitchy. "Today."

He reached across my desk for a Post-it note and scribbled something on it before tossing it down in front of me, grinning. "Meet me at my temporary humble abode two days from now at eleven p.m. sharp."

"I got it. Thursday night at eleven. I'll be there."

Oliver stood and came around to my side, clapping me on my shoulder. "See ya soon, cuz."

CHAPTER 4

SOMEONE CLEARED THEIR THROAT, and my body jolted. "Sorry," I threw the word over my shoulder, and moved forward in line.

"Can I get the sprinkle pop, mama?" Maisie asked from my side looking up at me with her father's electric blue eyes and a pleading expression on her face. I hated to deny her since it wasn't often that I was able to splurge on extra. Plus, she'd been doing well in her new pre-school, and I had mentioned I'd get her a special treat to celebrate. A quick check of the time said it was early enough not to spoil dinner or having her bouncing off the walls before bedtime. At least I'd hoped it was.

"Sure, baby. Ms. Nickels told me that you helped pick up all the crayons after your color time today. Thank you for being a good girl."

"I love to color. Purple is my favorite." She swung our connected arms forward and backward.

"Mine too." We took another step to reach the counter.

"Hi there. What can I get started for you today?" The barista asked.

"Can I get a medium regular coffee with cream and sugar, a small hot chocolate with a small cup of ice, and one of those pink sprinkled cake pops, please?"

"Of course, can I get a name?"

"Michele."

I paid for our purchase and then went to find us a seat. Ines should be here soon. It had been far too long since we'd seen each other, especially with my new, inconsistent work schedule. I'd thought working out in the real world would have far more regular hours than when I'd danced at *Sweet SINoritas*, but that wasn't even close to being the case.

It was the double shifts that were killing me, and I found myself working them more often than not trying to save money. Except, with the extra cost of paying for a sitter, I wasn't sure the long hours were even worth it.

The barista called my name, and I hurried to get our drinks, my eyes frequently darting back to Maisie, even though she wasn't more than ten feet from me. No sooner did I return to our table than Ines came scurrying across the coffee shop with a wave, her other arm weighted down by a baby carrier.

"Hey, I hope I'm not late. Who knew babies needed so much shi—stuff?" she quickly corrected after a glance in Maisie's direction. She pulled me into a one-armed hug and then turned to my daughter who'd jumped out of her seat to peer down at Zoey.

"Hey ya, Maisie May."

"Hi, Miss Ines," she answered, not taking her eyes off the baby. She was completely infatuated with the infant.

"Sorry," I said with a laugh. "You're second string now."

"I've gotten used to it," she said with a shrug. "Everywhere I go with her she gets all the attention. It's a good thing I love her, because she's killer on the ego."

"Tell me about it. Come, sit down. What do you want?" I asked.

Ines put the carrier on the seat next to Maisie. "I can go get it."

I waved her back. "You can get it next time. What do you want?"

She narrowed her eyes at me in playful annoyance, but I only smiled. "Fine. I'll take a small caramel macchiato, please. I should probably get decaf, but I'm splurging today."

"Eh, live a little," I winked at her and left her with my baby-obsessed child. Ines adored Maisie. She'd extended the offer to babysit multiple times if I ever wanted to go out on a date sometime, but I'd always turned her down. For starters, no one was knocking down my door *to* go on a date.

The only place I'd ever gone without Maisie was *Sweet SINoritas*, and the clientele there was hardly dating material. Two years ago, it was owned by a cartel leader, Miguel Álvarez. After it was seized, shut down, and then reopened under a new owner, most of the clientele were married men in their sixties who were unhappy at home or trying to relive their youth. Not that I was dancing there anymore.

Second, I was extremely careful about who I brought around my daughter. Especially after Jonas. I shuddered thinking about him. I picked up Ines' order and headed back to the table where Maisie was playing a rousing game of peek-a-boo with Zoey. I smiled at their laughter.

After setting the drink in front of Ines, I took my seat next to her and added a couple ice cubes to Maisie's hot cocoa. We'd learned the hard way how hot it actually was. Although it was probably pointless considering it would be cold by the time she got around to drinking it. Her focus was elsewhere. I turned back to Ines. "So, tell me what's been going on with you lately? Have you decided if you're going back to work or not?"

She took a sip of her drink. "I still haven't made up my mind. Brody says we'll be okay if I don't, but I miss it."

That didn't surprise me. Ines loved being a cop. Her entire family—her brothers, her father, her father's father—are and were, all cops. It's the only thing she'd ever wanted to be. It was in her blood. I couldn't blame her for missing it.

"I know your career meant a lot to you," I said.

I tried to imagine missing something that bad. Until two months ago, the only job I'd ever had was as a stripper. It had been the one thing, as a seventeen-year-old high school drop out with a fake ID, that I'd been qualified for. I loved the money I made, that was for sure. I'd earned enough to put myself through nursing school, pay for a sitter, and put a roof over my daughter's head. It would be a lie to say I didn't miss that part of it.

I hadn't loved taking off my clothes for strangers, putting up with the occasional groping, and certainly not the catty bitches I danced with. Well the few catty bitches anyway. I'd made a couple of close friends, and I did miss them. Mostly though, I missed the money.

"I don't have to make a decision today." She tried to

shrug it off. "What about you? I can't believe you've finally gotten out of the club. I feel like you're all grown up now." She practically cooed the last part. Not that Ines was wrong. Here I was, on the edge of turning twenty and just starting my first job in the real world.

My eyes danced over to check on Maisie, who was still busy having a one-sided conversation with Zoey about the field trip her preschool had taken to the library yesterday.

"Very funny. It's...different, that's for sure. Well, mostly different. I'm still dealing with the occasional grabby hands," I chuckled. "But for the most part, the residents are great. Who'd have thought that one day I'd be a nurse? I've still got a ways to go until I get my Bachelor's, but at least I'm out of *SINoritas*. Man, if my parents could see me now," I mused.

They'd be horrified actually. I was never meant to be the hired help, which is exactly what they considered a caretaker to be.

Doctor.

Lawyer.

CEO of some *Fortune 500* company.

Trophy wife.

My parents would have taken any of the above. Preferably the last. All the things I could have been. All the things I *should* have been. If only I hadn't gotten knocked up at fifteen.

"I'm so happy that things are going well for you. You've worked so hard these last three years, going to school and taking care of Maisie. If anyone deserves good things in life, it's you." She reached over and squeezed my hand. I had to swallow the lump in my throat. Life was a

27

daily struggle, and had been for years, so to hear her praise made me feel a little better.

"Thank you. I appreciate you saying that."

Just then, Zoey started to fuss. Maisie blinked a few times and her lips turned down. She looked like she was about to burst into tears right alongside the baby. Ines scooped her daughter up out of the carrier, and while she adjusted her shirt and pulled out a nursing blanket, I turned to my daughter.

"Here, eat your sprinkle pop, baby, and drink your cocoa before it gets any colder."

"Sorry," Ines said once she'd started nursing and the baby settled. "I meant what I said though. You should be proud of what you've accomplished. Anyway"—she patted the table—"tell me about the new place? Any problems? I know you're an adult and have been on your own a long time, but I worry about you two. Especially in that neighborhood."

Ines wasn't the only one. It made me a little nervous as well, but I'd needed something central to my work, Maisie's preschool, and her sitter's house that was actually in my price range.

"It's fine. I mean, it's not West Loop or anything, but it's convenient." I paused, debating on whether I should mention it or not, because knowing her, she was going to mother hen me to death. Before I could change my mind, I blurted it out. "There is this guy, though."

Ines perked up, a sly smile on her face. "A guy? Tell me more."

My nose wrinkled, and I shook my head. "No, definitely not that kind."

She straightened in her seat, her gaze locked on me. "I

don't like that look. Is everything okay? You're not in trouble, are you?"

Of course she was worried. The last time I'd had a problem, it ended in a drug war where Pablo had been shot. I lived with the guilt of that every day. If I hadn't asked Brody and Preston for help after my friend OD'ed at the strip club, he'd still be hale and healthy.

"Michele?" her voice was sharp.

"Sorry, no, I'm not in trouble. It's probably nothing." Having started the conversation, I felt silly. Like I was blowing something way out of proportion.

"If you're worried about it, then it's not nothing," she said, as though reading my mind. "Always trust your instincts, girl. What's going on?"

She wasn't going to let it go. Not that I blamed her. She was a cop, after all, and protecting people was ingrained in her. Ines was one of the only police officers I trusted. Her father and brothers were the others. The rest were useless and didn't give a shit about people like me. I'd learned that firsthand more than once over the years. To them, I was nothing but a slut. A whore. Trash, as I was called once.

I leaned closer and lowered my voice not wanting Maisie to hear. Thankfully, she was busy finishing off her treat. "He lives down the hall. Ever since he moved in, he's been constantly trying to hit on me. Telling me how well he takes care of his women and maybe he could take care of me. He's never tried anything. There's just something about him, you know? I've seen him hanging out front a few times talking to some pretty rough looking guys. "

Ines' expression was full of a combination of worry and anger. "Shit, Michele. Let me talk to Pablo. That's his precinct. Maybe he can talk to that guy. If need be, he'll put a stop to it. You have to be careful. Especially with Maisie."

The thought of Pablo knowing the kind of neighborhood I lived in bothered me more than it should. I'd never been ashamed of what I'd done over the last four years to not only take care of my daughter, but to actually survive.

But Ines was right. This wasn't just about me. I had my daughter to think about.

"I appreciate you talking to him for me. It's probably completely unnecessary. I'm sure the guy is perfectly harmless." There was an undertone of uncertainty in my words, and judging from Ines' skeptical expression, she heard it.

Maisie started getting antsy. It was time to go. "We need to do this more often," I said. "As soon as I get on a regular work schedule, we'll make a plan."

"You got it. Oh, before I forget, we're having a birthday party for my niece, Cristina, next week. If you're off work that day, you and Maisie need to come by for some cake and ice cream. I'll text you the date and time and just let me know."

"Thanks, we'd love to come if I can make it happen."

We packed up our girls and hugged goodbye. Maisie leaned in and kissed Zoey on the cheek. On the drive home, I kept thinking about Pablo. Despite the reason for him checking in on me, I was looking forward to seeing him again. Which was ridiculous. I was a twenty-year-old former stripper with a nearly four-year old kid who was barely making ends meet. What would he want with someone like me anyway?

CHAPTER 5

"Is your leg still bothering you?"

I flinched at the gently-asked question and glanced over at Ines. "Why do you say that?"

Her eyes flickered downward, and I followed the path of her gaze. Quickly I dropped my hand.

"You've been massaging it for the last five minutes. I know the doctor cleared you to return to duty and you're back to work, but are you really ready?" She reached out to clasp my fingers in hers. "You were shot Pablo. No one would fault you for taking more time off."

I bit back the sharp reply. Ines sounded like Peterman.

"It's just a dull ache. Must be a change coming in the weather." I laughed stiltedly releasing myself from her hold. "They say you can feel rain coming after a broken bone."

Ines stared hard at me, but thankfully didn't call me on my shit. Especially considering it was the middle of summer, and they hadn't forecast rain for several weeks.

"How are things over at Thomas Brothers, P.I. firm

31

doing? Brody and Preston still keeping busy?" I hurriedly changed the subject. My sister could never resist talking about her significant other and his brother's business.

She heaved a sigh but let the subject of my injury go. "They are actually. Brody doesn't share a lot of details about his cases with me—confidentiality and all—but he and Preston seem to be as busy as ever."

"Good. I know it's a far cry from the undercover work he was doing with the DEA, but it's definitely safer. I'm glad he hasn't gotten bored with it. Being a PI is a completely different animal."

"Are you kidding? After spending five years deep undercover and nearly being killed after his cover was blown, my fiancé is perfectly content with boring," she said.

"Fiancé, huh?" My brows raised. "Is this a new development? Because I'm pretty sure no one's said anything to the family."

"Then apparently everyone but you knows Brody and I are getting married. Hell, we have a damn kid. I think we've moved beyond the boyfriend/girlfriend stage at this point. We've all been a little too busy the last few months to think about a wedding. I may not have the ring yet, but he is still the man I plan on marrying. So, yes, fiancé." Ines nearly snapped the last word.

I held up my hands in surrender.

She might be six years younger than me, and the youngest in our family, but she didn't take any shit from me or our brothers. In fact, she didn't take shit from anyone. Best option was to diffuse the bomb before it exploded.

"Speaking of kids, when is that niece of mine going to

wake up from her nap? It's been too long since I've held her."

"Not before you leave, God willing."

Ines did look a little more tired than usual. "Zoey keeping you awake?"

"She'd been sleeping through the night, but then suddenly, a couple days ago, she started waking up fussy every two to three hours. Her appetite seems a little off too. I'm not sure what's going on, but I've got an appointment to see the pediatrician tomorrow."

"If you need the sleep, you know you can always send her over to our house. Dad would be happy to watch her for a night or two."

Ines laughed. "Dad, huh? I'm sure he'd appreciate you offering up his babysitting services while you're off with Oliver and your new undercover gig. How's that going by the way?"

"I'm as undercover as Landon was when she worked with Brody. Besides, you know I can't really talk about it."

Oliver was the one undercover. The one taking all the risks. I was just his handler. Except I couldn't shake this unsettled feeling.

"Promise you'll be careful. Oliver can be a little reckless at times. I already lost one brother."

The pain of Ernie's death hadn't lessened over the last two years. He'd been the eldest, and we'd all looked up to him. He'd been a good cop, the kind we all strived to be. And then in a single moment, he was taken from us.

"I promise. Believe me, I don't plan on getting shot again." I laughed, trying to lighten the mood. Ines didn't laugh with me.

"Don't even joke about that. You have no idea what

papá, Manny, and I went through when Victor called us that night." She choked up and tears filled her eyes.

"Hey," I said, pulling her into a hug. "I'm fine. A broken leg isn't going to keep a Rodriguez down for long. I'll make sure to keep Oliver in line. I'm his handler, that's all. Nothing is going to happen to me, okay?"

Ines sniffled and pulled back, grabbing a tissue from the box on the coffee table to wipe her face. "God, these stupid fucking hormones. I swear if I didn't know better, I'd think I was pregnant again."

"Are you sure you're not?" I asked.

She stared at me, aghast, cheeks still wet. "You shut your mouth right now, Pablo Ignacio Rodriguez. I can't believe you just uttered that blasphemy. I love Zoey more than anything, but fuck, there's no way I could handle two babies under the age of two at the same time. I'd go bat shit crazy."

Laughter escaped, and it actually felt good. It had been far too long since I'd felt like laughing. "I sure hope you clean up that potty mouth before Zoey learns how to talk."

"You're kidding, right?" Ines scoffed. "Between her four uncles and her father, my daughter is going to have a whole repertoire of dirty words to pull from. She certainly won't learn all of them from me."

That was the truth. Despite our best attempts, and Marguerite's scolding, we'd never managed to curb the swearing around Manuel's kids, Cristina and Nicholás. It was doubtful that anything would change with Zoey or with Victor and Estelle's little one when it arrived.

I couldn't believe how much our family was growing. A vision of a young woman and little girl popped in my head. I could still see the innocent gray eyes framed with long lashes staring up at me and feel the heat from her body when she'd laid her daughter in my arms. She'd been leaving here after a visit, and I'd carried a sleeping Maisie out to the car. It had been nearly four months since that evening, but the protective instinct that had flared to life hadn't dimmed. In fact, seeing them at the rec center the other day had caused it to surge back to life. *What was she doing right now?*

I blinked at the flash of movement in front of me. Ines waved her hand in my face. "Hey, I've been calling your name. You okay? You've been staring off into space for the last couple minutes."

"Yeah, sorry, my mind just drifted." I glanced at my watch and rose to my feet. "Thanks for the chat, but I should probably get going. I need to meet Oliver tonight."

Ines followed suit. She pulled me in for a hug. "Please be careful. Call if there's any trouble."

"I will. Everything's going to be fine though." If I said it enough times, hopefully it would be true.

"It better," she scolded fiercely, as though daring it to be anything other than what she demanded, and I couldn't help but smile. "Oh, real quick. Michele has been having some trouble with this creepy neighbor of hers sexually harassing her ever since he's moved in. He really makes her nervous. I sort of volunteered your services. I'm hoping you won't mind stopping in and checking on her and Maisie a couple times a week, since your precinct house isn't too far from her. She doesn't live in the greatest neighborhood."

A thin film of anger came over me at the thought of someone bothering her. "I can do that."

"Thank you." Ines gave me another hug. "I don't have her exact address. Only that it's in Little Village. She's coming to Cristina's birthday party on Friday. You can get it then."

We said our goodbyes, and I spent the rest of the day feeling a mixture of anticipation and dread for tonight, as well as rage toward some unknown man.

CHAPTER 6

I TRUDGED up each flight of stairs of the rundown building I called home. Temporarily, I hoped, anyway. The bundle in my arms grew heavier with each step. Paint peeled off the smoke-stained walls. The lights that did work either flickered, threatening to go out any minute, or surged bright and then dim again, casting a jaundiced hue over everything. The constant smell of mildew filled the air, which I wasn't sure was any better than the skunky scent of weed. It was a step above the last building I lived, though, and how depressing was that?

God, my parents would die if they saw this place. My mother would anyway. She'd wrinkle her nose and cover her mouth with a handkerchief I swear she carried for just that over-dramatic purpose. Then she'd sneer and tell me she wasn't surprised I'd ended up in a place like this. My father would merely say my name in that disapproving tone he always used and shake his head as though I was nothing but an embarrassment to the family. Not that I cared what either of them said. They'd been dead to me for years. Just as I'd been to them.

There were times I imagined them knocking on my door. Begging me to forgive them. Welcoming me back into their house. I couldn't help myself. *Did they ever think of me?*

A quiet snore sounded in my ear from the little girl I carried. She was the reason my parents had nothing to do with me. My smart and beautiful daughter. The absolute love of my life. We only had each other, and everything I'd done over the last four years had been for her. I pitied them for the fact that they would never know her. Despite all the struggles, I wouldn't change a thing. Not the long days spent studying my ass off. Not saving every penny. Not even the aching feet that were killing me after just getting done working yet another double.

Carrying an almost four-year-old wasn't helping either. Especially a sleeping one. *When did my baby get so big?* I was changing her diapers just yesterday, but here she was, this little person who had so much personality.

The stairs creaked under our combined weight, and the sound echoed around us. I froze. My breath caught in my lungs, and my lids slammed shut, as if that would prevent anyone from seeing us. I prayed that everyone stayed behind their closed doors. Silence reigned and my breathing began again. I resumed the climb, only my pace picked up.

I hurried down the hall toward my door. I breathed a sigh of relief until my ears caught the sound of hinges in dire need of oiling. *Shit.* I ignored the noise, stuck my key in the lock, and continued my prayer the whole time that I only imagined it.

"Good evening, little lady," a gravel-roughened voice bounced off the walls. "You're getting in awfully late tonight."

My hands shook. I shifted Maisie in my arms and pivoted to face the man standing far too close. The man I couldn't ignore. Not unless I wanted more problems than I was ready to deal with.

"What do you want, River?"

"Now, is that any way to greet a friendly neighbor? Someone who's only concerned about your safety? You never know what kind of riffraff might be roaming these halls at night."

Friendly neighbor my ass. River was nothing but a slimy wannabe gang member. I was tired and cranky and really didn't want to deal with his shit right now, but I also needed to be careful. River could continue to be a slight annoyance, or he could make my life complete hell.

"I appreciate you trying to look out for me, but I really just want to go inside and go to sleep. Like you said, it's late."

With his colorfully-tattooed arms crossed, he propped his lean form against the wall next to my door, emerald green eyes scanning up and down my body. There was nothing sexy about what I was wearing, yet the look in his eyes said he was imaging what lay beneath my clothes.

"You need a man to help take care of you. To treat you like a queen." He sucked his bottom lip between his teeth, letting it go with a pop.

God, I was so tired of his sleazy innuendos.

"I have a man." The words escaped before I could stop them.

River straightened and narrowed his eyes. "Oh really?"

No backing out now. "Yes, really."

"And where is this so called man of yours then?" His head swiveled around like he was actually looking for him.

Despite the heavy weight I carried, I rose to my unimpressive full height. "I don't think that's any of your business."

"Mama?" Maisie raised a sleepy head.

I rubbed her back. "It's okay, honey, go back to sleep."

She trustingly laid her cheek against my shoulder again.

"I'm taking my daughter inside now. Good night, River," I said, staring him down with a false bravado. My heart pounded inside my chest at his silent stare.

"Bring him by sometime. I'd love to meet the lucky man. Remember, though, if he can't satisfy you, I can help with that." He winked and finally turned to head down the hall and back inside his apartment.

I sagged with relief and let out the breath I'd been holding before turning the key in a hurried rush and then closing us inside. I threw the deadbolt and secured the chain. Dropping my bag on the floor, I toed off my shoes and made my way through the dimly lit living room and down the hallway to the bedroom. Multiple night lights illuminated my path.

Thankfully, Maisie remained asleep as I settled her in bed, pulling the covers up and around her. I dropped a gentle kiss to her forehead before pulling the door nearly closed. Exhaustion threatened to overwhelm me, and I'd wanted to do nothing but crawl in bed with my daughter, but my empty stomach pushed me to the kitchen.

While I stood there eating some cold, leftover pizza, I

looked around my tiny, one bedroom apartment. I'd piece-mealed all the furniture together. The clean, but faded to almost pink, second-hand couch was pushed up against a wall. It was bookended by mismatched end tables, and a clear glass lamp minus the shade stood centered on the one in the corner.

Cable was a luxury I couldn't afford. The rabbit ears on the box television stood at odd angles, each metal antenna pulled out to capacity, looking as though it was desper-ately trying to touch the ceiling. I was constantly having to fiddle with them to reduce the static on the four channels we could even get in.

I'd tossed down a few colorful throw rugs to try and cover the threadbare carpet and brighten up the place. A chipped formica kitchen table with three wooden dining room chairs completed what minimal furniture I possessed.

One of these days, I was going to be able to move us to a decent place. I just needed to keep my eye on the prize. With a resigned sigh, I finished off my slice of pizza and dragged myself into the bathroom for a quick shower. I would have loved to take my time—privacy was limited with a child—but my alarm clock would be going off far too early. Instead, I was in and out, putting my sleep shorts and t-shirt on, and crawling into bed in less than ten minutes.

Maisie's quiet snores came from the pillow next to me. She'd been sleeping beside me her entire life. I really needed to get her a bed of her own, but we didn't have the room, and I was embarrassed to admit that I liked having her close. It was a reminder that we were a team, she and I, and that I wasn't alone. I had someone who loved me unconditionally, even when I screwed up. I'd never had that before she'd been born.

Normally, her soft breathing soothed me, but tonight, after yet another encounter with River, I was still a bit on edge. The reassurances to myself that he was harmless were all I had, despite the fact there were moments I doubted myself.

I couldn't believe I'd told him I had a boyfriend, but I hoped it would be enough to get him to leave me alone. If he thought there was a man in my life maybe he'd take the hint I had zero interest in him, no matter how much smarmy charm he laid on me.

An image of Pablo popped in my head. I wish I knew what it was about him that I couldn't stop thinking about. Yes, he was gorgeous, but good-looking men were every-where, and I had no trouble dismissing them. Was it because he was Ines' brother? Or maybe it was how sweet he was to Maisie. I couldn't trust that though. Not after Jonas.

Whatever it was, it was too late to try and figure it out tonight. Tomorrow would be here far too soon, and I had far too many things to worry about, like saving up my money so I could get out of this shithole.

CHAPTER 7

THE HOUSE WAS STIFLING. Family were the only ones here, but lately, being around all of them made it so damn hard to breathe. I wanted to escape to my room. *What the fuck was wrong with me?* Even since I'd been shot, something inside me had changed, though I tried denying it. A quick glance around confirmed everyone was busy getting ready for the birthday party. I took the opportunity to slip out the sliding glass door and onto the back deck.

I was also on edge, because I was waiting for a call from Oliver. The last time we'd met, he was waiting on confirmation of something big, but wouldn't tell me what it was until he knew for sure. He'd gotten deeper inside Los Lobos and closer to Morales. I warned him not to push too hard, but in typical Oliver fashion, he did what he thought would get him more intel, and to hell with the risks.

A light summer breeze blew in off the lake to keep the temperature decent, but the humidity was thick. It wouldn't be long before the beads of sweat would grow above my lip. I didn't tolerate the heat well. The swings on the jungle gym Dad had installed after Cristina's birth swayed slightly back and forth. I leaned down on my forearms on the deck railing and sucked in a deep breath, the smell of my father's carne a la tampiqueña cooking penetrating my nose, and some of the tension eased out of me on my exhale. The department psychologist had cleared me to go back to work, but he'd cautioned me to take it easy. Not just physically, but mentally. I'd waved off his concern. I was fine.

The door opened behind me. My jaw clenched to hold back a sigh of annoyance at someone disturbing my solitude. Why couldn't I get a few minutes to myself without one of my brothers or sister interrupting me? All they did was ask how I was doing. Every fucking time I saw them. It was getting old.

"I brought you a beer."

The bottle appeared in front of me, and I took it from my father's hand. "Thanks. I thought you were cooking?"

"Brody took over."

I glanced sharply in his direction. "Brody?"

My dad chuckled. "Believe it or not, he's actually becoming quite the chef. I've been giving him a few cooking lessons on some of your sister's favorite dishes. You know that boy will do anything for her."

Envy coursed through me. I loved my sister, and Brody was like a brother to me. I was happy that they'd found each other. Both of my brothers had found love as well. Being around all the happy couples, though, was a constant reminder that I was alone. The last single Rodriguez. I took a sip of my beer to try and distract myself from those thoughts.

"Did I ever tell you about the time I was shot during a domestic disturbance call?"

Once again my head snapped in my father's direction. "What? When did this happen?"

He didn't look at me. Instead his gaze stayed focused out across the backyard. "I'd been on the force for five years. In fact, it was a week after my anniversary. My partner and I were out on patrol when the call came in about a couple yelling and a child screaming in a neighborhood on the southwest side of the city. We arrived on scene and knocked on the door announcing ourselves. More banging and yelling came from inside and then a male voice hollered that he was going to kill the woman."

After tipping back his own bottle for a drink, he continued. "We called for backup, but we couldn't wait until they got there. I kicked in the door and after a short scuffle we had the husband subdued. I'd just slapped the cuffs on him when I heard this loud pop, and then felt searing pain in my arm. The man's wife started screaming at us to let him go. By this time, backup had arrived and the woman was placed under arrest as well."

Jesus. All these years ... "Why didn't you ever say anything?"

My father shrugged. "I guess I never really thought about it. Being shot has always been a hazard of the job. Something all you kids already knew going in. It could happen to any of us. My point is, I know what you're going through. I've been there. It's not always easy to come back from it."

I stiffened. "Look, I told you all I'm fine. Like you said, it's a hazard of the job. I just wish everyone would stop talking about it."

Dark brown eyes everyone but me had inherited bore into mine. "Pablo, you are my son. I know each and every one of my children far better than they think I do. You can tell us all how well you're doing, but I see you. I see the way you limp and rub your leg when you think no one is watching. I'm not saying you should take it easy, even though you should, but you need to stop lying. Especially to yourself."

With a final disappointed look, my father returned to inside the house, leaving me with the echo of his words. *Fuck.* There was nothing I hated more than letting my dad down. The sick feeling in my gut only grew. I chugged down the rest of my beer and remained outside a few minutes longer.

The hustle and bustle of a full house remained as I stepped back into the dining room. Brody was still standing at the stove, and my sister-in-law was pulling something out of the fridge. Cristina and Nicholás went tearing through the den, whooping and laughing, and disappeared down the hallway.

"Oh, Pablo, can you please get in one of those grocery bags over there and find the candles for the cake?" Marguerite waved in the general direction behind where she stood. With a sigh, I tossed my bottle in the garbage and rifled through the plastic on the counter in the vicinity she'd pointed until I found a box of red, blue, yellow, and green striped candles.

The jingle of the doorbell rang through the house.

"Somebody get the door, please?" Marguerite hollered out over her shoulder.

The bell rang again.

"I'll get it," I offered and headed that way. Where the hell had everybody run off to?

The shadowy figure on the other side of the frosted glass fidgeted. I could see the erratic movement of whoever stood behind it. I pulled it open, and the air left my lungs. For several beats, I could only stare at the young woman standing there. Our eyes locked, hers widened in surprise.

"Hi, Mister Pablo."

I jerked at the greeting, and my gaze darted down to meet Maisie's. She was smiling and a completely different child than the one I'd first met outside the pool.

Thankful for the interruption, I smiled back at her. "Well, what a nice surprise. How are you? I didn't know you were coming."

If I had, maybe I could have prepared myself better. As it were, I felt like a nervous teenager on his first date.

"Mama said we was coming to a birthday party and there was going to be cake and ice cream and punch and maybe even games to play and I never metted 'tina before," she rambled, barely taking a breath.

Michele winced. "Sorry, she's just really excited."

Why was she apologizing?

"It's fine. Come in." I stepped back to let them by, and the soft scent of orange citrus wafted around me.

"Um, is there a place for presents?" she asked.

I cleared my throat and pulled my gaze away from her face to instead focus on the small package wrapped in pink paper she held in her hand. I glanced around. *Where the hell had Marguerite put the gifts from the family?*

"You made it. I'm so glad." Ines' voice filled the room. She hustled over, gave her friend a hug, and then bent down to pull Maisie into her embrace next before rising again. "Here, let me take that."

Michele passed over the gift.

"Come on Maisie May, why don't we go find Zoey?" She took the little girl's hand. "Pablo, maybe you could give Michele a tour."

I glared. *Was this some ploy?* Ines merely smiled, turned, and the two of them disappeared down the hallway toward the family room, leaving Michele and I alone in an uncomfortable silence.

CHAPTER 8

I stood completely dumbfounded, my mind spinning like mad. Ines had said cake and ice cream. I'd assumed we'd been invited to a kid's party, not to a family gathering. Oh, god. Was Ines playing matchmaker? No, she couldn't be.

"Would you like something to drink?"

My head jerked in Pablo's direction, but it took me a beat to process his words. Drink. Oh, yeah. "Sure. I mean, yes, please."

I really hoped he meant something with alcohol—the stronger, the better—because I was feeling the need for some liquid courage. Being near him gave me that fluttery sensation in my belly I hadn't experienced in a long time. And any time the sensation hit, it always seemed like I lost the ability to think clearly.

"Kitchen's this way," Pablo gestured, and I followed behind while he led the way.

Unconsciously, my eyes dropped to his ass. I'd gotten a pretty good idea what the front looked like, thanks to those wet swim trunks he'd been wearing a couple weeks ago, but the backside remained a mystery.

Holy hell was it worth the wait. His jeans displayed the taut muscled globes to perfection. My eyes were so focused on that really nice butt, I almost collided with it when Pablo came to a stop. Heat flared across my face, and I took a quick step back with a mumbled apology. *Quit acting like some sex-starved lunatic for god's sake.*

"Hey, Michele," Brody greeted me, and I sent him a silent thank you for calling attention away from my idiocy.

"Hi, there." I'd grown fond of him over the last couple years.

"We've got beer, pop, or water," Pablo said.

No vodka or tequila then. "Pop, please."

"Glass?"

"No, thanks."

He handed me the ice cold can, and our fingers brushed, causing a small current to flare to life. It felt so hot against my skin, I was surprised the aluminum in my hand didn't explode from the heat. My eyes met his, but he didn't give any indication he'd felt it too. Of course he didn't. Why would he?

"We'll just be in the way if we hang out in here much longer. Would you like to go outside? Or if you'd rather, we can go find the rest of the gang. They're probably all in the family room so be prepared for utter chaos in there."

A small sliver of guilt pierced me at the thought of not checking to make sure Maisie was doing okay, but Ines would come get me if there was a problem. Plus, I found myself really wanting to spend time with Pablo. He was probably only being polite with the invitation, but I didn't want to pass up the opportunity to talk more with him.

"Outside would be nice."

He grabbed a bottle of water from the fridge, and we headed out the glass door onto the large wooden deck that looked perfect for family cookouts. Something scraped across the wooden surface, and I turned at the sound.

Pablo had pulled out one of the chairs from around the square table with an opened umbrella speared through the middle of it.

"It's a little cooler in the shade."

He pushed the seat in behind me and then took the one next to me, both of us staring out into the yard. A weird feeling came over me. No one had ever held a chair out for me before. Within seconds of us sitting, his phone rang.

"Sorry," he said with a sheepish grin, reaching into his back pocket. "I'm never off duty."

"It's okay." I smiled back.

Pablo glanced down at his phone, and the mirth faded from his lips. In fact, his whole demeanor changed. Tension pulsed off him. "Excuse me, I have to take this."

He jumped up from the table without another word and hurried inside. I sat for a few minutes, debating on finding Ines and Maisie, and just as I made the decision to head in, Pablo opened the door and stepped back out onto the deck. He seemed different than before the phone call.

"Is everything alright?"

Pablo's head jerked in my direction and he blinked like I'd pulled him from a distraction. "Hmm? Oh, yeah, it's nothing. Just work."

Pablo didn't elaborate, so I cleared my throat to break the silence, plucking at the tab on the top of my can of pop. "I don't think I ever thanked you."

His head swiveled in my direction, brows furrowed. "For what?"

"For the whole *Rapture* thing and going after Mr. King for supplying it. I mean, you basically got shot because of me. I'm sorry you were injured because of it, but you have no idea how relieved I am that my friend got justice. I only wish that you hadn't been hurt because of it."

He should resent the hell out of me.

"I appreciate it, but none of it was your fault." Pablo shifted, his expression flickering with some emotion, and glanced away as though uncomfortable. Whether for my gratefulness or my apology. Maybe both.

"I know, but I still feel guilty about it."

Call it a flaw, a failing, or even a weakness, but I've always felt bad about things I have no control over. Didn't matter what it was. My mother lamented over it constantly. She'd always tell me to never show regret. Guilt was a wasted emotion. She said it was for the weak. Things happened. You dealt with them, and then you moved on. No need to wallow in could haves or should haves.

"Ines told me that you're having problems with one of your neighbors?" Pablo changed the subject.

The same feeling that I was blowing this out of proportion came over me. I didn't really want to talk about River. I also didn't like the idea of anyone fussing over me. I'd gone my entire life without anyone but my daughter caring about me. It was difficult remembering the fact that I had friends who wanted what was best for me. "I'm not sure I'd call it problems, really. He's just a little flirtatious, I guess. I try to ignore him when I can."

"I assume you have sturdy locks on your doors and windows?"

"There's a deadbolt and chain on the front door. I'm on the fourth floor, so I haven't really paid attention to the windows. There's no fire escape, and I don't have a balcony, so unless they rappel from the roof, no one should be able to get in."

"That's good. Make sure I have your address before you leave, and I'm more than happy to swing by and check on things a few nights a week. I've got things going on in the area, so I'm almost always nearby."

The thought of seeing Pablo more often was certainly an appealing one, but I hated to inconvenience him. He must have sensed my hesitation, because he laid a hand on my arm.

"I'd feel much better about your and Maisie's safety if you let me do this."

For a moment I couldn't say anything. All I could do was feel the heat of his touch on my arm. It dashed across my skin and then settled like a warm puddle of straight whiskey deep in my belly. I raised my eyes to meet his, and my heart rate kicked up a notch. My tongue darted out to wet my dry lips. His gaze flickered to my mouth, and there was a flash of arousal in his expression.

The sliding glass opened, startling me, and Pablo quickly pulled his hand back.

"Food's ready, you two," Ines announced from the doorway, a twinkle of mischief in her eyes. "Be sure to save room for cake, though. After we're done eating Cristina is going to open presents."

"Thanks," Pablo said, drily. "We'll be right in."

She disappeared back inside, leaving the door open.

"I guess we better get in there before the mob shows up and all the food disappears," he joked.

Awkwardly I rose and headed inside. The back of my neck tingled, as though his eyes followed me. Chaotic noise greeted me. The kitchen was full of every Rodriguez and their extended family members. It was standing room only. I hadn't made it two feet into the house before Maisie barreled into me, wrapping her arms around my legs.

"Mama! Mama! 'tina let me play with her dolly and we colored and I drawed you a picture." She drew back, shaking the piece of paper in her hand. "Lookie."

"My goodness, you've been busy haven't you? Let me see what we have here." I took the page from her, glanced down at the picture, and blinked. "Wow, look at all these people. Who is everybody?"

She pulled my hand down that held the paper and started pointing. "That's Miss Ines. And that's Zoey. And that's me."

"Who's this?" I indicated the two stick figures that seemed to be holding hands.

"Mama," she drew out the word like she was exasperated I couldn't figure it out. "That's you and Mister Pablo."

There was a cough, or maybe choked laughter, from somewhere, and mortification swept over me. Today was only the second time she'd even met him. I needed to say something.

"Thank you, sweetie, it's wonderful. You did such a good job. I'm going to hang this on the fridge when we get home."

"Can I see that?"

The question came from directly over my right shoulder. I turned my head and was nearly nose to nose with Pablo. His eyes met mine for a moment before he moved his gaze to the drawing still in my hand. I passed it over to him. He seemed to study it intently, before he nodded his head. His attention then went to Maisie. "This, young lady, is a masterpiece. Thank you for including me. It's beautiful."

To my amazement, she giggled and blushed. Apparently I wasn't the only one affected by Pablo.

"Alright, everyone," Ines' father, Ernesto, called out. "Let's get eating."

It was obvious the family had a system when they got together to eat. We all formed a line and slowly inched forward until finally Maisie and I got to the food. I made us both plates and followed the crowd. We all settled inside the family den where one long table that seated twelve for the adults and one small card table for the kids were set up.

I settled Maisie next to Cristina and slid nervously into the seat beside Estelle, Ines' best friend and future sister-in-law. At first, it was awkward, while everyone chattered about family stuff since I had nothing to contribute, but eventually my body relaxed and I tried to enjoy myself. Ines always made sure to include me in the conversation. Through the entire lunch, I was acutely aware of the man seated across from me.

CHAPTER 9

Fᴜᴄᴋɪɴɢ Oʟɪᴠᴇʀ. It had taken all I had to return to Michele and act like everything was okay, when in fact it was far from it. He and I had set up a code phrase to indicate when we needed to meet face to face. He'd sneak in the time and place, which was typically not for a couple days. We also had one when it was an emergency. During our brief conversation he'd used the emergency phrase, which meant we needed to meet tonight.

My attention throughout the meal had been divided between why Oliver would need to see me ASAP and trying not to be obvious about watching Michele. Finally, I pushed work out of my mind since there was nothing I could do until later, and focused on her.

She'd been quiet, hesitant, at first, but as time wore on, she opened up and was soon laughing at Victor and Manuel's antics. My gaze kept coming back to her again and again. There was a sharp kick to my leg beneath the table, and I hissed under my breath at Ines.

"What the hell?" I mumbled out the side of my mouth.

"You're staring." She leaned over and whispered back.

I turned my head toward her and her eyes darted in Michele's direction and back to meet mine. Thankfully the other woman was busy talking kid stuff with Estelle, who taught elementary school, and didn't notice she was the subject of discussion.

"I am not." Okay, so maybe that was a lie, but I didn't need Ines pointing out the fact.

She smiled and stuck out her tongue. "Are too."

I rolled my eyes at her.

"You should ask her out," she said.

My food got sucked down the wrong pipe, and I coughed and choked to clear it. Half the table's eyes landed on me, and I waved off everyone's attention. I grabbed my water and took a drink.

"Excuse me?" I was going to regret asking her to repeat herself, but I was obviously not thinking straight.

"You heard me. I saw your reaction to her when she first got here. Then, inviting her outside with you. The two of you were looking pretty chummy when I came out to get you. Hand on hers. It was cute."

Only Ines would jump to the conclusion that I needed to ask Michele out based on a single touch. She did the same thing with Victor and Estelle. Granted, she'd been right about them being in love with each other, but still.

"Even if I was interested"—I tutted when she opened her mouth to speak—"*if* I was interested, I'm too old for her. I'm sure she has no interest in a guy my age."

She stared at me without a word. Just stared. Then, she smacked me alongside the back of my head. Conversation around the table stopped and everyone stared at us, Michele included.

"Ow," I said, rubbing it. "What the fuck was that for?"

The rest of the family took it in stride if the multiple eye rolls were an indicator, but the woman across from me looked around like she was in a house of lunatics.

"Children," our father chided from the head of the table. "We have a guest. Can you at least try to be on your best behavior? For a little while anyway. Please?"

"Sorry, papá," Ines said in a soft voice seemingly chastised.

I echoed her apology, but with less contrition. I hadn't done anything except get smacked. Finally the din of conversation rose again as everyone returned to their discussions. I turned to Ines, the back of my head still smarting. She packed quite the wallop for someone her size.

"Why did you hit me?"

"Because I was trying to smack some sense into you. You are not too old for Michele. You're mature and stable. Something that poor girl has never had in her life."

Mature and stable? Good god, she might as well have said I was middle-aged. "I have to have at least fifteen years on her."

"So? And by the way, I think it's only fourteen."

What was the difference? "I'm sure she has plenty of guys, younger guys, she can go out with."

"She doesn't, actually."

I hated the fact that I cared. "How do you know?"

"Because she told me. I don't know why you're so against it." She paused. "She's smart, ambitious, kind, and an amazing mom. Unless that's something you hold against her."

"Of course I don't," I said, ignoring her narrow eyed glare.

"I can't figure out why you won't ask her out. I call bullshit on the age thing."

There wasn't a chance in hell I was going to say this to Ines, mostly because I didn't want to get smacked again, but I was afraid to ask Michele out. What if she said no? Worse, what if she said yes? I was thirty-four years old, and I'd never had a single long-term relationship. I couldn't remember the last time I actually went out on a date. A glance at Ines told me she was still waiting for a response.

"I'll think about it." I needed to say something to satisfy her, although I doubted that would for long.

Her lips pinched.

"I will."

She let out a huff. "Fine, I won't push."

I snorted. Pushing was what Ines did best. Especially when she thought she was right. Luckily I didn't earn myself another pop to the head, although she did pinch my side under the table. I rubbed the sore spot.

Everyone finally finished eating. Victor and Manuel picked up half the dishes while Estelle and Marguerite picked up the other half. The four of them took everything into the kitchen and started loading the dishwasher or washing things by hand.

"Wow, I don't think I've ever been to a dinner like this where the men help clean up?" Michele had come to stand next to Ines, who laughed.

"We were a family of five boys and a girl. We don't follow the weird, unwritten rules that seem to say that women should cook and clean up after their men. Plus, I don't think either Landon or Estelle would put up with that. They're both far too independent for that misogynistic crap. In our family, men and women are equal partners."

The amazed expression remained on Michele's face. *What kind of family did she grow up in that she was so surprised by this?* My curiosity ran rampant. Damn Ines for putting the idea of asking Michele out in my head. I couldn't stop thinking about it.

"Mama?" Maisie appeared at her side. "Can I go outside with 'tina and play on the swing?"

Michele glanced over at us with a question in her eyes. Ines looked around. "We're going to be a while cleaning everything up and putting the food away. Plus we need to let lunch digest before we can dive into cake. The kids can play for a while. Burn off some energy."

"I'll go out with them," I spoke up, causing the two women to turn to me. I avoided Ines' gaze.

"Thank you," Michele said to me before turning to her daughter. "Yes, sweetie, we can go outside."

"Yay," Maisie hollered and then raced across the room yelling even though my niece was standing right there. "Let's go swing, 'tina."

The three kids took off through the house with cries of excitement.

"We should probably get out there before they start fighting over who gets which swing," I said.

I ignored the wink Ines sent my way, thankful that Michele hadn't seen it. The two of us once again headed outside. We took our previous spots at the table. The sun had finally moved behind the house, so I closed the umbrella. I didn't need the wind they were calling for tonight to catch it and overturn everything later.

Maisie crawled up into the swing and Cristina was pushing her gently while Nicholás climbed the miniature rock wall. My eyes darted to Michele sitting next to me. A small smile graced her face as she watched the kids play. We sat silently, while I racked my brain trying to think of something to say. It was times like this that I wished I was more like Victor— he could talk to any stranger he passed on the street.

I cleared my throat nervously. God, I hated this awkwardness. "So, Ines tells me you just graduated nursing school."

Michele pulled her eyes away from the kids and focused on me. I felt the punch of her attention hard. "I did. Well, with my LPN anyway."

"LPN?"

"Oh, sorry," she said, abashed. "Licensed practical nurse. It's a stepping stone to becoming a registered nurse, which is my ultimate goal. I wanted to get out of *Sweet SINoritas* as soon as I could so I got the fastest degree that would help me get my foot in the door somewhere. I'm working in a nursing home while I keep studying for my Bachelor's."

It couldn't be easy with a fulltime job, going to school, and being a mom. "That's really great. You're juggling a lot and seem to be doing it well."

She laughed with a little head shake that seemed self-conscious. "I don't know about that, but thank you for saying it anyway."

"I mean it."

"Well, thank you."

Several screeches made us both jerk our heads in the kid's direction, but they were laughing and running around the yard chasing each other. Michele continued to watch them while my leg bounced and my fingers tapped the table.

"Would you like to go out for coffee tomorrow?" I blurted out. *Smooth, Rodriguez.*

The question hung in the air.

"Mama! Mama! Look at me," Maisie hollered. Both Michele's and my attention jerked to her daughter who was almost to the top of the nearly six-foot rock climbing wall.

CHAPTER 10

OH, shit. Heart pounding, I took off running down the deck and across the yard, Pablo right behind me. My voice caught in my throat, but I didn't want to yell and startle Maisie. We reached the jungle gym at the same time my daughter pulled herself up onto the platform. She turned, her smile huge, and waved down at us in glee. My heart continued beating with the speed of hummingbird wings, and I willed it to slow. She was fine.

"Mama, did you see me climb?" She was bursting with excitement at her accomplishment. I didn't want to scold her for scaring the hell out of me, because of how proud she was of herself.

"I did. You climbed so high. I'm glad you were careful. That looked scary." I smiled to soften my words.

This was a side of Maisie I'd never seen.

She rolled her eyes. "It wasn't scary. It was fun. I want to do it again. Mister Pablo, catch me."

Before I could blink, she jumped off the platform and right into his arms. He caught her with no effort at all.

Maisie laughed. The second he set her on the ground, she was back to the wall, her fingers grabbing, and her feet moving, from rock to rock as she made her way back up to the top. She had no fear. Twice more she did it, and twice more he caught her. His niece and nephew joined in. No sooner did her hands touch the wall for a fourth time than Ines hollered from the open doorway.

"Who's ready for cake and ice cream?"

All three kids screamed, "Me", in unison and took off toward the house, leaving Pablo and me standing there. Tiredness settled in my bones from just that short bout of play, and all I had done was watch the kids jump and shout. What continued to amaze me was how Maisie responded to Pablo.

"Well that was fun," he said next to me.

I didn't sense any sarcasm in his tone.

"I'm so sorry she just kept jumping on you like that."

Those eyes of his studied me, his head tilted just slightly off center. "Why do you always seem to apologize for the things Maisie does? Or things you do, for that matter?"

"Sorry."

"Like that."

I winced, and attempted to meet his gaze again, although it was more his right ear that my eyes landed on.

"It's just a bad habit I haven't broken, I guess." Which made me feel ashamed. I didn't need to apologize for Maisie. Not ever. I needed to do better.

"The only way that could have become a habit was if there was someone wanting you to apologize in the first place," Pablo said.

This time, I did look him full on. He didn't appear

happy. In fact, there was a tightness around his mouth, his lips pinched. Almost as though he were angry.

"There was this guy I used to date. Turned out he didn't like kids." I shrugged. "Or maybe he just didn't like my kid."

"He's a fucking idiot."

I blinked at Pablo's vehemence.

"Maisie's a great kid, and you don't ever have to apologize to me about anything she does. Not if she talks so much she barely takes a breath. Or if she jumps off a jungle gym a hundred times and wants me to catch her each one. Not ever. Understand?"

Words stuck in my throat. Jonas had seemed like such a good guy at the time. Charming. Kind. He'd treated me really well, and I lapped up his attention. At first, he and Maisie seemed to get along, but little by little he was nagging about her being too loud. Too messy. Too annoying. Every time, I kept apologizing, like she was the problem and not him.

I finally managed to nod.

"Now, before they send out a search party to drag us in for that cake and ice cream, you didn't answer my question from before."

How could I have forgotten? A new hyper awareness of the man standing next to me tickled my senses. His smell. The heat of him despite the warmness of the air around us. Just the sound of his breathing hitting my ears. I replayed his question. Coffee? With him? Tomorrow?

"I'm sorry, I can't tomorrow."

"Sure, no problem." His lips barely tipped up on one side. "Is there another day that works better for you?"

I racked my brain trying to picture my calendar in my

head. Tomorrow was a double. Sunday regular. Monday? Monday? Was I off Monday? Crap.

"Monday might work, depending on what time. I'll have to check my work schedule just to make sure. I also have to check with Maisie's sitter. I mean, if that fits your availability." I stumbled over the last, because I just assumed that he'd be able to make it.

Thankfully, he didn't take offense. "My schedule is probably a lot more flexible than yours. Why don't I give you my number? Call me once you know your schedule for Monday. If that doesn't work, maybe we can try another day?"

My cheeks felt hot, and not just because we were in the middle of summer. "Okay."

"Great. You ready to head inside? If we're lucky they may have left us a sliver of cake."

"Yeah, I should probably check on Maisie. No doubt she's bargaining her way to more dessert. She got her sweet tooth from me, I'm afraid."

"That's good information to file away for the future. If I ever need to bribe either one of you, I know your weakness now." Pablo waggled his brows with a devious smile that gave me a whole lot of dirty thoughts. He didn't need to bribe me to do anything. All he'd have to do is look at me the right way, and I'd do almost anything he asked. But the fact that he was speaking of the future sent a shiver racing through me.

I needed to bring it down a notch though, and not read into things. I mean, he was Ines' brother. No doubt we'd run into each other again at some point in time. He probably didn't mean it the way my wishful thinking brain interpreted it.

We strolled side by side back to the house. I almost swore his hand brushed mine once, but it didn't happen again, so I more than likely imagined it. But the heat from just that brief touch stayed with me through cake and the opening of presents. Before I left, Pablo gave me his number, and I gave him my address. Then I thought of nothing else on the drive home but calling to confirm our date.

CHAPTER 11

IT CAME as no surprise that the minute Michele and Maisie left, Ines cornered me. I'd stayed in the family room, picking up all the destroyed wrapping paper and shoving it in the garbage bag, hoping for a few minutes of privacy. It was dumb of me to think it would last long. Within two minutes, Ines strolled in trying to look innocent and failing.

"You and Michele sure spent a lot of time together today."

"Don't you have anything better to do than stick your nose in my business? I'm sure Brody or Zoey need you for something."

"Nope," she said with an exaggerated popping sound. "They're both doing just fine. You on the other hand…"

"I'm doing just fine, thanks."

"Ohhhh, do tell." She sat in Dad's recliner, leaned back, and crossed one leg over the other as though she had no intention of going anywhere. Which, knowing Ines, she didn't. Not until she'd weaseled every bit of information out of me.

With a sigh, I stuffed the last bit of paper in the white, plastic bag, and turned to her. "Since I know you're going to nag me to death, I asked her out."

That had her sitting up straight and practically bouncing in the chair. "And?"

"And she had to check her work schedule."

Her smile drooped a bit, but then the corners turned back up. "So it wasn't a no?"

"It wasn't a no." I held back my own grin.

"This is so exciting. I knew you two would be perfect for each other."

I held up my hand. "Whoa, let's take it down a notch here. We haven't even gone out yet. There's nothing that says it will go past coffee. Besides, you know what it's like trying to date and be a cop. Not everyone can handle it for a lot of reasons."

Ines waved me off. "Michele is made of stronger stuff than any of those other random chicks you dated. They weren't girlfriend material."

A little offended at her words, I narrowed my eyes, ignoring the implication that Michele *was*. "Random chicks? Really? Some of them were very much girlfriend material, thank you."

Her lips pursed in distaste. "Then they would have lasted longer than a date or two, wouldn't they have?"

I appreciated the fact that my sister seemed to think it was the women that were the problem and not me, but it wasn't fair to them. "You know, maybe they had a good reason for not wanting to commit to something long term. Did you ever consider that maybe I was wrong for them and not the other way around?"

"Of course. You're my brother, so I know that you're far from perfect. Like far, far from perfect."

"Excuse me," I sputtered.

"What? It's true. But so are the rest of us. We all have our faults. But I also know all the good things about you. The biggest thing about you is that you love with everything. If those women had been worthy of you, you would have put your all into it. So, if it didn't work out, it was because they didn't do the same thing."

Wow. Was what Ines said true? All this time, I'd decided my shitty love life was my fault. I worked too many hours. My job was too dangerous. I was too picky. Or maybe there was something wrong with me. I wasn't good looking enough. Wealthy enough. My family took up too much of my time. Looking back, there were definitely women who no doubt thought that. But more often than not, it was something about them that always held me back from putting forth the effort to make things work.

"I guess I'd never thought about it that way."

With Michele, it was different. *She* was different. There was this vulnerability beneath the surface that I wanted to protect. She presented a strong front to everyone. She had to. She had a daughter to raise, and she did it by herself. That required a strength and resilience far beyond what people understood. My father had that same strength. It hadn't been easy for him to raise five kids by himself, but he did it. Ernesto, Manuel, and I helped as much as we could, but it wasn't the same. It was probably harder for Michele because of her age, and because I was pretty sure she didn't have anyone to turn to for help.

"Like I said, you two are perfect for each other. And because I love you and want to see you happy, I'm going to give you a piece of advice. Never, ever, lie to her. There's nothing she hates more than a liar. I want Michele to be happy as well." Ines rose from her seat and patted me on the cheek. "Don't fuck it up."

I'D LEFT the house and was on my way to meet Oliver down at the Navy Pier. It was a huge tourist attraction and far enough away from his apartment in Little Village that the chances of someone from Los Lobos seeing us together were slim. I hadn't forgotten his call from earlier today. Since all the excitement of the day had finally settled, my brain shifted into work mode.

I made a quick stop at the coffee shop for an Americano before weaving in and out of the crowd, making my way down the pier like I was just another visitor. It was peak summer vacation season. Normally, the crowds didn't bother me, but every bump and nudge from the warm bodies surrounding me made me more and more twitchy. I couldn't wait until this conversation ended so I could get the hell out of here and back home.

My gaze darted back and forth through the throngs of tourists until finally, I spotted Oliver standing near the press box and ticket booth. I shouldered past a cluster of people and made my way over. About six feet from him, his gaze met mine. He jerked his chin in greeting.

"Thanks for coming."

I took a sip of my coffee and glanced around, taking in

everyone, checking for eyes and ears. "What was so urgent that you needed to see me?"

"Maria Luis Valesquez," he said under his breath.

Shit, no wonder he'd been in a rush to meet.

"What about her?" I took another drink, trying to settle my nerves.

"There have been rumblings through the grapevine. Bits and pieces of intel. Nothing solid, but vague references of an alliance."

"Between?"

"Valesquez and Morales."

Jesus Christ. If she was making some type of arrangement with the leader of Los Lobos, was she planning something against her half-brother? Trying to get El Diablo to turn traitor?

"Can you find out to what end?"

"That's what I've been working on. She despises Salazar and has been doing everything she can to take away his power. If she succeeds, she could potentially take over the whole Sinaloa Cartel."

This was huge. This was also something the DEA needed to know if they didn't already. "Let me talk to my contact with the Feds. See if she's got any further intel. After Álvarez and King, Valesquez is on their watch list. It isn't every day that a woman becomes the most powerful drug smuggler in Mexico."

"I'm going to keep my ear to the ground and see if I can't get one of Morales' lackeys to give me more," Oliver said.

"Don't push too hard. This isn't all fun and games. You could compromise the whole investigation if you blow your cover. Worse, they could kill you."

75

He scoffed and patted my shoulder in a placating gesture. "I swear that bullet did more damage to your balls than it did your leg. Stop worrying so much."

I jerked out from under his touch. "As your handler, it's my job to worry. Especially considering how reckless you can be."

Oliver's eyes widened and he gestured to himself. "Me? I'm the reckless one? You seem to forget who dove into the Chicago River after a suspect tossed a bag of drugs in there. Or who ran headlong into the Thanksgiving float parade to continue a foot pursuit. Oh, yeah, and who's the one who didn't wait for cover in the middle of a drug raid and got himself shot because he was trying to be a hero? Don't talk to me about being reckless, you damn hypocrite."

"And look where it got me?" I yelled back. The crowd around us all stared in our direction, and I stepped closer, lowering my voice. "It was *because* I was careless that I got shot. Which is why I'm telling you to be careful. I could be dead right now, and so could you. You know what? I'm done here. Call me when you have more news."

With that, I spun, slammed my empty coffee cup in the trash, and elbowed my way through the crowd. Away from this place.

CHAPTER 12

THE DOOR to the locker room swung open again, and another nurse filed in. Excitement filled the air, mostly because their shift was over, and it was time to head home. I, on the other hand, vibrated with emotion for an entirely different reason. As soon as I left here, I was going to meet Pablo for our date.

I stared at my reflection in the dust-covered mirror, leaning in to get a closer look while I applied a little more mascara. Since I quit dancing, I'd stopped wearing a lot of makeup. But I'd been told that it made me look a few years older, so I figured it couldn't hurt. Not too much, but enough that Pablo wasn't reminded of how young I was. After I finished applying my eyeshadow, I dabbed my lips with a pale pink gloss. It would disappear after a few sips of coffee anyway, but at least I'd put some effort into looking nice.

"Where you going that you're getting all dolled up?" My co-worker, and the first friend I'd made after I started working here, Gretchen stood behind me. She was old enough to be my mother, but she had a youthful vibe to her that made her seem more like a sister. Or at the least the cool aunt every girl wanted.

"I'm meeting a friend for coffee."

"Please," she said with a once over between my freshly brushed out hair, makeup, and the slightly more than casual outfit I'd changed into. "All of this tells me your so called 'friend' is a guy."

My cheeks filled with heat.

"Fine. Yes, it's a guy." I turned to face her. "But, it's just coffee."

Gretchen rolled her eyes. "A woman doesn't pay this much attention to her appearance for casual. So, spill the tea. Who is he?"

I moved a few steps and settled on the bench in front of a row of lockers while she dropped next to me with a grin that said she was ready for all the juicy, or in this case not so juicy, details.

"His name's Pablo."

"Ooh, Latino. Is he muy caliente?" She fanned herself like she was having a hot flash. "That's the extent of the Spanish I remember from high school."

"He's gorgeous," I sighed. "He has the most beautiful hair I've ever seen on a man. It's a little on the longer side and he wears it all messy with these kind of dark, wavy curls that dip down over his forehead and his ears. I just want to brush them back and run my fingers through it. And don't get me started on his eyes. They're the color of warm honey, and every time he looks at me it's like they penetrate right through me and see all the way to my soul."

"Lord almighty. Do I need to get the fire extinguisher

and hose you off? Hell, you might need to hose me off. I'm totally jealous. He sounds delicious."

He really was. "It's more than just his looks though. There's something about him that makes me feel safe, you know? And god, he's so good with Maisie."

"That's the thing you gotta watch for when you're a single mom. How they treat your kids."

Didn't I know that? I'd experienced disappointment with that before.

"Does he have any hot brothers?" Gretchen waggled her eyebrows. I only shook my head, because she was happily married to her high school sweetheart and had been for the past eighteen years.

"Sorry, both his brothers are already taken. He's got a huge family. I'm friends with his sister, and they're all really close. I've never been around people like them before. They would do anything for each other. No questions asked."

"Well, I hope you have a great date. I can't wait to hear all about it, because you know I'll be asking the next time I see you. Old married women like me need to live vicariously through young people like you," she said.

"Whatever. You're hardly old. Anyway, I should probably get going. I have to meet him in about thirty minutes, and you know how traffic can be heading downtown." I rose, grabbed my makeup bag from the counter and pulled my purse from my locker before locking it.

Gretchen waved as I headed out of the locker room. "Don't forget to use protection," she called out just as the door closed behind me. I sputtered out a laugh and glanced around hoping no one else heard her. Good grief, this was one date for coffee.

Nearly twenty-five minutes later I was pulling into the parking garage a block from the coffee shop. It was a little mom and pop place that had been around longer than I'd been alive. The sun shone down from the cloudless sky and cast a bright glare off the Chicago River. I loved coming into downtown. Everything was so big and busy down here. People were always walking around exploring all the city had to offer.

I reached the entrance and stepped through the front door, the cool blast of air hitting my face. My eyes scanned the interior and quickly met Pablo's gaze. I waved and mouthed a 'hey'. He returned my smile with the one of his that made my insides gooey and rose from his chair to greet me.

"Hi. I'm glad you could make it," he said.

For a second, I froze, not sure if I should shake his hand or reach out for a hug. I had no idea what the protocol was for a coffee date. Luckily, I didn't have to decide, because Pablo wrapped his arms around me. Mine circled the middle of his muscular back. The hug only lasted for three or four seconds, but his scent surrounded me, and I breathed in sandalwood mixed with just a hint of…chlorine maybe, like he'd just been at the pool. There was also a subtle aroma that I guessed was all Pablo. He pulled back and gestured toward the table.

"Why don't you have a seat, and I can grab our drinks. Unless you need to look at their menu."

I sat in the chair opposite the one he'd vacated. "No, I'm good. I'll take a regular coffee, please."

"Any cream or sugar?"

"Black," I said with a shake of my head.

"You got it. I'll be right back." He turned and headed to the counter to place our order.

Of course, I watched him the entire time. It had been almost two years since I'd been out on a date, and I was rusty. Not that I'd had that much experience with it in the first place. And the track record I did have wasn't saying much for me either.

After Jonas, I hadn't trusted my judgement with men enough to dip my toes back in the dating pool. Yet here I was out on a date with a guy that I was almost sure was a good one. Or maybe just too good to be true.

No, don't do that. I wasn't going to compare Pablo with my experiences with Warren or Jonas. This time I was going to go slow. Make sure that my instincts weren't playing tricks on me just because he was beautiful. Outer beauty often hid inner ugliness. My mother was a prime example.

Pablo returned with our drinks and sank back down into his chair. "How was your day?"

"It was uneventful, thank goodness. Which is actually a good thing when you work in a nursing home. A slow day is a good day."

"I can relate to that. A slow day for me is a good day as well. That means I'm not busting down doors, chasing people while they dump things out of their pocket, or getting shot at."

The last made me wince. I'd tried to hide it, but I must not have succeeded since Pablo reached across the table and touched my arm. "Hey, I'm sorry. I didn't mean it like that. It's something that happens more often than I'd like, so I promise that wasn't directed toward any single incident."

It made me feel better hearing him say that, but then I felt like a jerk that it made me feel better. I couldn't imagine someone shooting at me, not just once, but multiple times. "That has to be tough on you. Knowing that you could be trying to arrest someone and they start shooting."

"It comes with its challenges. Since I work in narcotics, we always know going into a bust that it could turn violent. Usually things go down peacefully, but the bigger dealers have the most to lose so they fight the hardest to protect themselves and their product."

"Like Mr. King?" I asked.

"Exactly."

"Do you enjoy it? Being in narcotics, I mean?" I took a drink of my coffee, savoring the roasted flavor.

Pablo mirrored me and brought his drink to his mouth. He didn't answer for a second. Instead he plucked at the lip of the paper cup. The hesitation took me by surprise. I'd expected him to answer with 'of course.' But it seemed like maybe that wasn't the case.

Finally he spoke. "I do. At least I think I do. Or I did, anyway. I reveled in the excitement of my job. I got to put bad guys away, and there was this rush when I did. I'll even admit I was a little cocky. Except lately, I feel like everything is different. That I'm different."

"What changed?" I asked softly, unsure if I should continue a topic that had turned a lot more serious than I'd expected.

He rubbed his face. "I got careless. I went into a raid thinking I was bulletproof. I underestimated the suspects, and in return, one of them shot me. Ever since I started back to work last month, things aren't the same.

I'm not the same. It's just made me question a lot of things."

I sat there stunned. On one hand, the guilt over him being shot kept threatening to rear its head. While on the other side of it, Pablo admitted that him getting shot was because he didn't take proper precautions. That bit of information did a lot to ease the sense of responsibility I continued to feel despite all his protests to the contrary.

"That must be hard. Questioning everything you'd done before. I understand that completely. There are so many things I've done in the past that I analyze, over and over, wondering what I should have done differently. My mother, despite being the most un-motherly woman known to man, and a rotten human being to boot, actually shared a piece of wisdom that has stuck with me. She said that the mistakes of our past shape and mold our present. But that doesn't mean we can't break the mold to change our future. I always took that to mean that the person I am today because of mistakes I made in my past doesn't mean I can't become a different, better person tomorrow by learning from them. I'm sure she meant something completely self-serving, but that's how I choose to interpret her words."

It was Pablo's turn to sit silently. I held myself still instead of fidgeting. He was probably thinking what a terrible person I was for speaking ill of my mother. I tried to not ever talk about my parents, but sometimes things like that slipped out.

"I think that's actually a pretty accurate interpretation. It makes me feel a bit better. Thank you for that."

"You're welcome." I ducked my head a little self-consciously. I'd never taken compliments well. I always felt awkward. A compliment coming from Pablo made me fluttery for other reasons.

"Well that was probably the deepest discussion I've ever had on a first date," he chuckled trying to ease some of the tension in the air.

"Me too."

"I guess that means we'll have to keep it much lighter on our second one. I know this one isn't even over yet, but I'd really like to see you again. Maybe for dinner? I'm a pretty decent cook. You and Maisie could come over one night. If you'd like that is."

There went that pitter-patter again. "I'd like. I mean, that would be nice."

"Good. Now that we got a lot of the serious stuff out of the way, how about we talk about something much better? Like, what's your favorite food? I want to be prepared for date number two."

For the next half an hour we talked about superficial things like what was the last movie each of us saw. It was Avengers: Infinity War for Pablo and some made for television movie I couldn't remember the name of for me. If we were Cubs or Bears fans—baseball had been something I'd enjoyed watching with my grandfather before he'd died, so I was a Cubs fan for life, while Pablo said since they'd grown up in Colorado he was more a Denver Broncos fan. What the best view of the city was—Willis tower or the Centennial wheel—we both agreed hands down on the latter.

I'd discovered that while he had a great sense of humor, he also tended to be a little on the more serious, quiet side. I avoided all conversation about family while he regaled me with antics from his childhood. He'd looked up to Ernesto, his eldest brother, but still felt somewhat apart from the rest. Ernesto had Manuel, while Victor had Ines. In a sense, he'd been an only child like me.

"I've had a great time today," I said.

"Me too. I meant what I said about dinner. I'd really like it if you and Maisie wanted to come over one night this week or next if you're free."

I smiled a little shyly. "I've got a huge test I'm studying for on Thursday, but we could come over one night after that."

"Fantastic. I won't bother you while you're studying, but how about I call you Friday and we can pin down a day?"

"That sounds great. Well, I better get going. I've got to pick Maisie up from the sitter's before five-thirty." I rose from my seat and Pablo was right on his feet as well.

"Where are you parked?"

"I'm in the garage over on the next block." I pointed in the direction I was headed.

"That's actually where I am too. If you don't mind me walking with you?"

I hadn't been ready for the date to end, so I didn't mind getting to spend a little more time with Pablo, even if it was just for a short walk to the car. "Not at all."

Together, we headed toward the parking garage, an occasional comfortable silence falling between us. I couldn't remember ever feeling this at ease with a guy, especially not on the first date. But with Pablo, once I'd gotten over my initial nervousness, everything had gone smoothly. He was easy to talk to, and the more time I spent with him, the more I was certain he really was one of the good guys.

"This is me," I said, stopping in front of my ten-year old Honda Civic that had seen better days. It was an eyesore. But it got me where I needed to go, so I didn't care what it looked like.

"Be careful driving. Traffic leaving downtown is going to be a beast," Pablo cautioned.

"I will. You as well. Thank you again for a really nice time. I'm looking forward to dinner."

"Me too," he said. Before I could guess his intent, he moved closer, brushed my hair off my forehead with his forefinger, and pressed his lips against it.

A shiver raced down the back of my neck, and the heat of that single touch sizzled through my body. He pulled away and his eyes flickered downward to my mouth and back to my eyes. I held my breath waiting to see what he'd do next, but he slowly took a step back. I almost whimpered.

"I'll call you after Thursday."

"Okay," I whispered back.

He turned and walked away, but before he disappeared around the corner, he looked over his shoulder one last time. I remained frozen until he was out of sight. Then I nearly melted with a sigh of bliss. Just that brief touch of his lips against my skin, and I was utterly infatuated.

CHAPTER 13

I HADN'T HEARD from Oliver since Friday. Normally, I wouldn't be too concerned, but after our conversation and how I'd left it between us, as well as his tendency to take a lax approach to things, I was a bit on edge. I was also waiting on a call from my DEA contact. I'd brought Oliver's intel about Valesquez to our Captain so he'd be in the loop if one of us managed to get further details.

After finishing up the last pending report on my desk, I shut down my computer and grabbed my keys. My desk phone rang just as I rose from my chair to head home for the day. I considered ignoring it, but knowing my luck, it was important.

"Rodriguez."

"It's Landon. I got your message. What's going on?"

Definitely important. I'd worked with Landon on two separate occasions. The first was when Estelle had been kidnapped by Miguel Álvarez. The second on the King case.

"Do you guys have any recent intel on Maria Luis Valesquez?"

"How recent?"

"Recent enough to include any rumblings of something going down between her and Ricardo Morales?"

"Not that's come across my desk. I'm taking it you have?"

It was nice having a contact inside the DEA, especially one who didn't think she was too good to work with those of us at the local level. It helped that she was part of my extended family. She was engaged to Brody's brother, Preston, which practically made her my sister-in-law. Or something. Either way, Landon Roberts was family.

"Possibly. We've got an undercover agent inside Los Lobos. He and I met a few days ago, and according to him, there's a rumor going through the gang of some type of alliance between the two of them. I don't know how accurate it is though."

"Shit. Let me talk to Brickman and Crawford. They're working Sinaloa, so they might have heard something. I'm skeptical of any type of alliance. Morales is making a significant amount of cash from that relationship. With that kind of backing he's going to think twice about giving it up," Landon said.

She was right. *El Diablo* would be hesitant to interrupt the amount of cash flow his gang was getting from Salazar.

"Unless Valesquez offered him more. You guys said yourself that she's made some powerful connections and allies during her rise to power. Everything she's done has been to fuck over her half-brother. Hell, she murdered Álvarez's first supplier and took over his entire business.

She's smart. Now that Salazar has control of Chicago, my guess is she's pretty pissed. I'd be surprised if she didn't have some grand plan brewing."

Landon sighed on the other end. "Let me do some checking. I think we have a guy inside. I'll see if his handler can reach out to him and find out anything. Give me a week or so and I'll get back to you."

"Alright. In the meantime, if I hear anything on my end, I'll call."

"Thanks, Pablo."

I collapsed back into my chair, blowing out a frustrated sigh. There was nothing I could do right now until Oliver contacted me again. This was one of the moments that I was conflicted. I was an action person, not a sit around and wait for things to happen person. But I also didn't want to rush into something and cause potential damage. We needed to be cautious, because one wrong move could fuck everything up.

Knowing it was pointless to keep waiting here, I grabbed my keys from where I'd dropped them when Landon called and headed out to my car. It wasn't long before I was pulling into the driveway next to my father's vehicle. The smell of something delicious reached me the second I opened the door. The whole family joked that I still lived at home because I didn't want to give up Dad's cooking. Victor had only moved out a few months ago when he shacked up with Estelle.

The quiet had taken a bit of getting used to. For so long, it had been papá, Victor, Ines, and me. Then Brody entered the picture and my little sister was suddenly all grown up. The two of them had gone into hiding in Colorado after his DEA cover within the Juarez Cartel had been exposed a couple years ago. Once the dust settled and Álvarez was dead, they'd come back to Chicago, but they found their own place. That left just our father and me.

"Hola, papá," I called out, shutting the door behind me.

"Hola, mijo." My father stepped into the den wearing his usual apron. I'd threatened to get him one of those tall, white chef's hats if he wasn't careful. "Come, help set the table, please."

We both headed into the kitchen where he made a beeline back to the stove. I reached into the cabinets and grabbed our plates and glasses.

I finished putting out the place settings and filled up our glasses with water. "Can I help with anything?"

"No, thank you. I'm about finished here. Why don't you have a seat and tell me about your day. Or, better yet, what about your date with Michele?" He asked with a hopeful smile over his shoulder. He'd always told us that his greatest dream was for each of his children to find the kind of love he and our mother had. She'd been gone for twenty-eight years and in that time I'd never known him to look at another woman. He said she'd been his one true love and it wouldn't be fair to someone knowing our mother still held his whole heart.

I wasn't sure I was ready to talk about Michele, or our date, but for some reason my mouth opened and words started to spill out. "It was really nice. We met for coffee at Schwartz's downtown. We talked about more serious things than I ever have on a first date. She's a great listener. Surprisingly more mature than even some of the women my age. Of course, she's had to be."

"Raising a child on your own is not for the weak. That girl has a strength forged from steel. I think that she will be good for you."

"You sound like Ines," I said.

"I saw the way you looked at her when she was here. That little girl of hers too. Those two are special and I think they'd fit right in with this family."

"Jesus, now you really do sound like your daughter. I swear the two of you already have us married. Maybe we should see how the first few dates go. Even then, I'm pretty sure it's far too soon to be talking wedding bells."

"It takes but only a moment for the heart to know. I knew I loved your mother the first time I saw her."

I'd heard their story so many times as a kid. They'd shared it over and over, and unbelievably, we never got tired of hearing it. We saw how much they loved each other.

"I'm not sure it's quite that instantaneous in this case. We're just getting to know each other. Taking things slow."

My father turned, skillet and potholder in hand, and placed them in the middle of the table. He hung his apron on the hook next to the pantry and then took his seat across from me. Neither of us spoke while we dished out our food. We weren't two minutes into eating before he set down his fork. "Perhaps it is good that you're taking things slow. You need to be careful. Especially with that little girl being part of it. That was also one of the reasons why I chose not to date after your mother died. Being an instant mother, or father, is no easy task. There is so much to navigate. Do you know if the father is in the picture?"

I shook my head. "Not from what Ines has said, but

91

then again, I'm not exactly sure how much she knows about Michele."

"That is something you need to think about. If the father is part of the equation, then how will you deal with that? You won't be Maisie's dad. You'll have to be sure you don't come between that relationship if there is one."

"I would never do that. If Maisie's dad is in her life, then he would always remain there. I don't need to compete with some man for her affection."

"What about her mother's?"

"What do you mean?"

"I mean that the two of them have a child together. She must have cared about him at some point. They have history."

"I think any woman I've dated in the past has had history."

"True. But where are all those women now?"

He really did sound like Ines. I wasn't sure why Michele was different from any woman from my past, but she was.

"What is that look on your face about?" he asked.

I blinked. "Huh? What look?"

"You had this expression on your face like you were thinking of something unpleasant."

"I was just thinking about our age difference. There's quite a bit."

"Michele has enough life experience to give her plenty of age. It wouldn't surprise me if she hasn't seen more heartache and sorrow than you. From what your sister has said, her parents kicked her out of the house when she was only fifteen. She survived on the streets, alone, even after Maisie was born. That kind of life will age any person. I don't think that is something you need to be concerned about. Besides, I would think someone who matches her in maturity is something she is looking for. The young men her age wouldn't know what to do with her, or her child."

He was probably right. "I'll take your words into consideration. Now, can we be finished discussing my love life?"

"Of course. Just think about what I've said. Don't be concerned about anything other than how you feel about Michele and how she feels about you. The rest is inconsequential. Now, what about our friend, Oliver?"

Throughout the rest of our meal we talked about the news Oliver had shared and that I'd passed on his intel to Landon. My father agreed with me that the lure of money and power would be a huge incentive for Morales to turn on Salazar. After we finished eating and clearing off the table I headed up to my room.

I collapsed onto my bed and stared up at the ceiling thinking about my date with Michele, what my father said at dinner, as well as what I wanted for my future.

After ten minutes nothing was any clearer than it had been. I still wanted to spend time with Michele, getting to know her. I sat up, slapped the heating pad on my leg, and turned the tv on. Oliver's name flashed across my phone's screen.

"What's going on?"

"The pawn is in position to knock the king out of power. He's protecting the queen."

Fuck.

CHAPTER 14

I'D BEEN STARING at the clock for the last three hours. Actually, that was a lie. More like all damn day. I'd gotten through dinner okay, but afterwards Maisie had nearly thrown a fit, because I hadn't been paying enough attention to her coloring and the alphabet homework she'd been sent home with from preschool. My phone hadn't rung.

Maybe Pablo would call tomorrow. He said after Thursday, and it was only just Friday. I didn't want to believe that he'd lied and had no intention of calling me in the first place. I drew the line at being lied to. Even a white lie. Because small lies tended to turn into big ones. I'd rather have my feelings hurt by the truth than have someone speak an untruth.

I kept reminding myself of that brief kiss, even though it had only been to my forehead. It hadn't felt like a goodbye kiss. An I-don't-plan-on-seeing-you-ever-again kiss. It had felt like the beginning of something. Like a prelude. As though Pablo was just getting started with all the places his lips would touch before it was all said and done. I tried to focus on that train of thought and not let myself get led down the other path. The one that said maybe he wasn't as good a guy as I'd been trying to paint him.

I'd already put Maisie to bed. It had been well past her bedtime, and I'd needed to study a little more. The television was on, but the volume turned down low, and I was sitting on my faded couch with my pharmacology book open. After two chapters of rabid note taking, I set my book aside and stretched. I walked a couple laps between the kitchen and living room just to get my blood flowing a little.

I plopped back down on the couch and went to grab my book to go through one more chapter, when my phone rang. My stomach flipped. Taking a deep breath, I reached for it trying to calm my racing heart. I let out a small squee at the name on the screen, but quickly composed myself before answering.

"Hello?"

"Michele, it's Pablo. I hope I'm not calling too late."

"Not at all. I was just sitting here studying a little."

"Oh, I'm sorry. I didn't mean to interrupt. I thought your test was yesterday."

He'd remembered. "Oh, it was. I'm studying for a different one, but it's not for a couple more weeks. It's a tough subject so any time I can get a little extra reading in, I try to."

"If this is a bad time, I can let you go. Call back another time."

"Not at all. I was actually just taking a break anyway. My eyes were starting to cross."

"I guess I timed it right then. What are you studying?"

"Drugs, actually," I laughed at the near irony. "So, did you have a nice week?"

Pablo let out a rough sigh. "Not really. Although it's better now that I'm talking to you. I'm sorry I haven't stopped by to check on you. We've had some things going down with one of our undercover agents that's been taking all my time. Which isn't an excuse, since I promised I'd look in on you. I apologize."

"It's okay, I understand. You were doing it as a favor to Ines, but I know how important your work is, and that it takes priority over other things."

"It wasn't just a favor. I wanted to. Which means I should have made the time. Especially with what you said about your neighbor. Has he still been bothering you?"

"Surprisingly, I haven't seen him at all this week. Maybe he finally gave up after our last conversation and the things I said to him." I winced and slammed by palm against my forehead. *Please don't ask. Please don't ask.*

" What did you tell him?"

Shit. "I might have implied I had a boyfriend already."

"Oh, really?" Pablo chuckled. "And what was his response to that?"

"He didn't believe me. In fact, he seemed almost offended. Like it was a personal affront to him that I'd chosen someone else."

"Good. Keep telling him that. Feel free to use my name if you need to. Eventually maybe he'll take the hint. What time will you be home tomorrow? I'll make sure to pop in. If we're lucky, he might make an appearance. I'll put on a good show for him."

My heart skipped and a small tingle began low in my

belly at the thought of what Pablo meant by putting on a show. I let out a nervous giggle. "After four-thirty. But don't feel like you have to go through some big production. Maybe just seeing you will be enough to dissuade him from future flirtations."

"Believe me," his voice dropped even lower than normal. "It wouldn't be any trouble at all."

Oh, god, was he flirting with me? *Think of something flirty to say back.* "If anyone could make him feel insecure about himself, it would be you."

"What makes you say that?"

I gesticulated with my hands even though he couldn't see me. "You know, with all your muscles and that lovely hair of yours."

My mouth snapped shut, and I squeezed my eyes closed, dropping my head back against the couch. The filter from my brain to my mouth was apparently broke.

"You think I have lovely hair?" There was laughter in his voice.

"Please forget I said that," I begged.

"No way. I want to hear more about my hair. I don't think anyone has ever called it lovely before."

"Fine," I huffed. "Your hair was actually the first thing I noticed about you. I may have even mentally threatened bodily harm to anyone who dared to cut it."

"Wow, you really are fierce. Okay, I won't cut it except a trim every now and then. How about that?"

"What? No, you don't have to do that. I didn't mean it. It's your hair. If you want to chop it all off, then don't let anyone stop you."

"After that threat? I wouldn't dream of it. I'd be worried you'd hurt me."

I couldn't help but laugh at his ridiculousness. "You won't let me forget I said that, will you?"

"Not a chance." I imagined him shaking his head on the other end. How embarrassing.

"Do you want to know the first thing I noticed about you?" Pablo asked softly, almost seriously.

Nervous jitters filled me. Did I want to know? Yes. "What's that?"

"The adorable way you spoke—a mile a minute—apologizing to me for something that wasn't in any way your fault. You were so cute and nervous and truly sincere even though the apology was entirely unnecessary."

Cute? It wasn't beautiful, but I'd take it. "I tend to ramble when I'm nervous."

"I noticed." He let out a small chuckle.

There was a short silence before I spoke up again. "I worried you weren't going to call."

"Why would you think that?" he asked. It wasn't accusatory, merely curious.

All the men in my life had slowly ripped away every bit of my confidence, beginning with my father. Warren had been a mistake, but one I'd overcome after a while. Jonas, on the other hand, had been harder to get over, because he hadn't just hurt me, he'd also hurt Maisie. But, Pablo? Something told me that he had the capability of completely and irrevocably shattering my heart. And I wasn't sure I'd be able to recover from that.

"Where do I start? I'm a former stripper. I have a kid. How about the fact that there are so many more women closer to your age who have their shit together and who are doing more with their life than just getting by."

Nothing like laying my flaws out there for him to see. I

was sure there weren't two more different people than he and I.

"You remember that Ines was a stripper for a short time, right? Why would I hold that against you?" Pablo seemed genuinely confused.

"That was all for show, and she was only there for a couple months. I was there for almost three years. Do you know how many men saw me naked? How many men groped my ass or copped a quick feel of my tits? How many men I gave lap dances to?" The ugly truth wouldn't stop flowing from my mouth no matter how much I tried to hold it back.

Was I *trying* to sabotage this whole thing before it even had a chance to get started? The longer he was quiet, the more it sank in that I'd said too much. I'd ruined everything.

"I don't know your whole story," Pablo finally began. "Maybe one day you'll feel comfortable enough to share it with me. What I do know is this. You put yourself through school to give both you and your daughter a better life. It doesn't matter how you did it. You can't change the past. Nor can I. I wouldn't even want to, because your past is what made you who you are. And I happen to like who you are. A lot."

Through his entire speech my throat closed tighter and tighter and the tears began. For years I'd believed I was selfish for not giving Maisie up for adoption. To let people raise her who could give her a better life. Things I couldn't give her. What had I known about being a mother? I was a fucking kid. I had no idea how to take care of myself, let alone a baby. I'd done so many things wrong and felt like a failure.

"Michele? You there?"

"I'm here," I choked out. "Just a minute please."

Moving the phone away, I grabbed some tissues, wiped my face, and blew my nose loudly. Finally, I felt composed enough to talk.

"Meeting Ines and your whole family has been the best thing to ever happen to me. Which is kind of sad if you think about it."

"I don't think it's sad at all. I think it means that you've been on your own long enough and now you don't have to be. It's a good thing. You have us. You have me." He paused. "If you want to, that is. If that means we're friends, then we're friends. I hope it becomes something more. No matter what happens, though, you'll still have me."

Hearing Pablo say that only made me want to cry more. "I'd like that very much."

"Good, because I would too. I also meant what I said. Hopefully one day you'll share your story with me. I want to know everything about you. The good and the bad. You don't have to hide anything or shy away from sharing your past. I promise I won't judge you for any of it. You should be proud of everything you've done. You're an amazing woman."

"Thank you." Taking a deep breath, I continued. "If the offer is still open, I'd really like to have that dinner with you."

"Of course it's still open. When are you free?"

"Let me check." I leaned over and grabbed my pocket calendar from my backpack and flipped to the current page. "Is a weeknight or weekend better for you?"

"Either one."

"Okay, how about either Sunday or Tuesday if that's not too soon?"

"Why don't you and Maisie come over on Sunday around six? That will give me time to run and get groceries. While I'm thinking about it, is there anything either of you don't like? Or any allergies I need to worry about? I want to make sure to cook something you'll both enjoy."

My heart skipped at Pablo's thoughtfulness. He had a niece and nephew so he was probably used to kids being picky eaters.

"I'll eat anything. Maisie doesn't really have any dislikes. At least not from the food I've given her. To be honest though, we don't have very sophisticated palates." I laughed a little self-deprecatingly. We ate what I could afford and that wasn't usually anything fancy. If it was cheap, I bought it. Which meant we lived on a lot of processed and boxed foods.

"I'll make sure to keep it simple. Nothing too fancy. I can't cook as well as my father can, but I can certainly hold my own. And if you guys liked the food we had at the birthday party then we should be safe with what I've come up with."

"I'm looking forward to it. I'll admit I'm probably one of the worst cooks out there."

"Well, I'll be happy to teach you a few simple recipes if you'd like. We can sample a few things and see what the two of you enjoy."

"I'm sure whatever it is, it will be delicious."

"I hope so. I have two women to try and impress so I better make it good."

There went that fluttery feeling again.

"I know you're trying to study so I won't keep you any longer. But I promise, I'm going to swing by tomorrow after you get home and check on you."

"Okay, that sounds good."

"I'm sure she's already asleep, but tell Maisie I wished her a good night, and I wish the same for you. I'll see you tomorrow."

"Goodnight," I whispered.

"Night."

I disconnected the call and held the phone close to my chest as though to keep Pablo closer to me a while longer. The things he said about me continued to ring in my head. Was I not giving myself enough credit for all the things I've accomplished? Maybe I needed to take a good hard look at my life and see all the positives instead of focusing on the negatives. Because he was right. What I'd done in the past was over. I was making something of myself. I worked hard and provided Maisie with everything she needed. We weren't living on the streets anymore.

Glancing around the apartment, I took everything in. It wasn't a lot, but it was mine. Bought and paid for with my hard-earned money. A small sense of pride began to fill me. Maybe I was doing okay after all.

CHAPTER 15

AN UNEASY SUSPICION pulsed through me on the way to Michele's. I took another quick glance at the paper in my hand with her address written in pretty, flowing script just to confirm I was going to the right place. That feeling soon began to morph into pure, unadulterated rage the closer I got. It was possible I was jumping to conclusions, but my instincts were telling me I was right. My white-knuckled grip on the steering wheel tightened even further. I worried I'd break the thing, my anger was boiling so hot.

People milled around the streets. Kids dashed around the fenced-in basketball court across from Michele's building. I found a narrow parking spot a block down and maneuvered my car into the opening between a clunker with a trash bag covering the place where a side window should be and a tan sedan with a flat tire.

Please be wrong. My stomach burned from the acid churning inside it. I passed a graffiti covered building, the colors exploding across the stucco surface. In large letters

Los Lobos was prominently displayed with a gorgeous depiction of a howling wolf next to it.

The sun peeked out from behind the solitary cloud in the sky, shining down to brighten the neighborhood, as though trying to showcase what the place could be instead of what it actually was. But no amount of sunshine could soften the darkness lurking in the shadows of hidden alleyways and inside the run-down buildings of Little Village. To outsiders, the neighborhood was a pestilence. A blight on this great city of ours inhabited by drugs, gangs, and death. To the residents, it was home. Some by choice, others by circumstance.

My eyes panned upward taking in the building in front of me. The door opened with ease, the security lock long broken. Just like everything else around here. It seemed it was all broken down in some way. I didn't like the fact that this place was Michele's best option, but I also understood she was doing what she could to get by.

The stairs creaked under my feet, the sharp sound echoing around me. I paused on the landing of the fourth floor, debating whether to turn right or left. My eyes darted left down the far end of the hall, my gaze narrowing on the last door. My jaw ached from being clenched, and I wiggled it back and forth to ease the tension. The rational part of my brain told me to turn right. To cool off before I confronted the man behind the door at the end. But I didn't want Michele and her daughter to see the rage that most surely burned in my eyes.

Decision made, my feet pounded on the worn carpet. With a heavy fist I rapped on the door of apartment 427. An apartment I'd recently been to. The barrier opened a crack, and I shoved it the rest of the way. I pushed past the slack-jawed man inside.

"Close the door," I bit out between clenched teeth.

"What the fuck, Pablo?"

"Close the goddamn door."

Oliver's expression was full of confusion, but he did what I said. "Jesus, man, what's your problem? You're not supposed to be here."

It took everything I had not to punch him.

"Stay the fuck away from her. Don't talk to her. Don't even fucking look at her." I seethed with rage. I couldn't believe a man I called friend was a goddamn creep.

"Stay away from *who*?"

"Michele."

He continued staring at me, completely oblivious. *He didn't even know her fucking name.*

I jammed my finger in the direction of her apartment. "The young woman you've been harassing since you moved in." I ran my hands through my hair. "Jesus, Oliver. What the fuck is wrong with you?"

Finally, the confusion cleared, and he had the sense to look shame-faced. His gaze darted away from mine.

"I didn't mean anything by it. You know how I am. I flirt with all the women." He tried blowing off his behavior.

My disgust was evident in my sneer. "You don't flirt, Oliver. You creep. Your shtick of this smarmy predator has to stop. It's not attractive. You have this poor woman so scared that I'm here checking on her, because she thinks you might take your pathetic flirting game one step too far. You're not only a grown man, but you're a fucking cop. You're supposed to protect people, not terrify them."

"I didn't realize you knew her."

God, he just didn't get it. "It doesn't matter if I know her or not. She's a young, single mother living in a shitty neighborhood. She does not deserve having to put up with the bullshit you've no doubt said to her. You're under-cover, Oliver. You paying attention to her could be putting her and her daughter in danger. Did you even fucking think about that?"

He held up his hands in defeat. "I'll go apologize to her."

"No," I snapped. "I wasn't joking when I said don't talk to her. I'll let her know you won't be bothering her again."

With that, I stormed past him and let myself out. I didn't even want to be in the same room with him. If I thought it would make a difference, I'd ask the Captain to assign someone else to be Oliver's handler.

I was keyed up, and it probably wasn't the smartest choice to see Michele when I was like this, but I found myself in front of her door anyway. I'd promised I'd check in on her. Before I could change my mind, my knuckles connected with the wood. Faint footsteps came from inside and then she was in front of me, a bright smile on her face that quickly faded. I tried to force my facial muscles to move, but my jaw was clenched too tightly.

"Is everything okay?" Michele asked with a nervous hitch in her breath.

"Yeah. Can I come in?"

"Y—Yes, of course." She stepped back, and I measured my stride so I didn't storm past. My rage wasn't directed at her. I needed to rein it in.

The door closed behind her and she leaned against it,

her fingers twisting at her waist. She opened her mouth, but Maisie rushed over from where she'd been seated at the kitchen table and wrapped her arms around my leg.

"Hi, Mister Pablo. I didn't knowed you was coming over. Wanna come see what I got?"

Finally, I was able to unfreeze the rigidness from my frame. I sent what I hoped was a reassuring smile to Michele, who offered a half-hearted one in return, before I gave my full attention back to Maisie. "What do you have?"

She grabbed my hand and pulled me over to what looked like a puzzle she'd been working on. For the next few minutes I watched her put the oversized pieces together, her tongue peeking out between her lips in total concentration. Between each piece she rattled off all the things she did at preschool that day while I nodded, *ooh*ed, and *ahh*ed in the appropriate places, all the while keenly aware of the woman watching us.

Eventually, Maisie finished and must have decided that was enough show and tell for the day, because she jumped down from her chair and settled on the floor in the living room with her crayons and drawing paper. Michele came over and pushed the completed puzzle to the other side of the table and took the seat her daughter just vacated. "Have I done something wrong?"

"No," I rushed to reassure her. "I'm sorry if I made you feel that way. I hesitated coming over here feeling this angry, except I didn't want to break my promise. I want you to trust that I'll do what I say I will."

"Then what is it?"

I couldn't disclose Oliver's identity to a civilian. "If I could tell you, I would, but it's work related." I reached across and squeezed her hand, looking her straight in the eye so hopefully she could see the honesty in them. "You have my word that I won't ever intentionally hold the truth from you, but I also work with undercover agents, so there are things I can't talk about. This happens to be one of them."

She studied me, her hand slowly ceasing to tremble beneath mine. Finally she blinked and gave me a short nod. "Thank you for your honesty. I hope whatever happened to make you mad gets better."

I turned her hand over and rubbed my thumb gently over her palm. "I will always do my best to be honest with you."

We continued staring at one another until Maisie rushed back into the kitchen breaking our connection.

"Mister Pablo, read me a story?" She stood next to me and thrust a book under my nose.

"Maisie Danielle Lewis, what have I told you about using your manners? We don't demand things. We ask nicely," Michele corrected, her voice sharp.

I bit back my grin at the expression of chagrin that spread across the face of the miniature version of her mother. She looked properly chastised as she cast her gaze to the floor. "Sorry, mama." Then she laid those baby blues on me. "Mister Pablo, will you read me a story, please?"

"If you don't have time…" Michele began.

I waved away her concern. "It's okay. I think I have time for one story."

"Yay," Maisie hollered.

She snatched my hand and tried pulling me out of my chair. I let her and she tugged me along and out into the living room, directing us to the couch. Once I was seated, she climbed up next to me and handed me her book. I opened it up and began to read, her small head resting against my arm while she stared down at each page I turned.

I was acutely aware of Michele, who'd followed behind us. The only place left to sit besides the floor was on the other side of Maisie. She hesitated, but finally she settled in next to her daughter while I read about a young girl and her puppy.

CHAPTER 16

LISTENING to Pablo read to Maisie was both the sweetest and the sexiest thing ever. If I hadn't already been falling for him, it was watching the two of them together that put me over the edge. He was so patient with her, listening any time she had something to say, and it was obvious she adored him. I didn't talk about Warren with her, and she had yet to ask. With her being in pre-school and around other kids who had dads, it was only a matter of time before she did start asking though. Seeing Pablo with her made me realize that when the time came, I was going to have to come up with something. It hurt me that I had to tell her the truth. At least a sanitized, age-appropriate version of it.

I always thought I'd be enough for her, just the two of us as a team, but seeing Maisie blossom under the attention Pablo paid her, that wasn't fair. It was pretty clear she was doing well with a male influence in her life. Or at least with this man's influence. She certainly hadn't responded this way to any of the other men I'd briefly dated, and most certainly not to Jonas. It made me happy to see how animated she was becoming, but it also scared me. Because he was capable of breaking not one heart, but two.

"The end," Pablo said with flourish, closing the book and setting it down on his lap.

"Read it again, please," she begged.

"Maisie," I drew out her name. "Pablo said he had time for one story. We can't keep him here all night. He probably has somewhere he needs to be."

He shook his head. "I actually have the evening free. But I also don't want to impose by overstaying my welcome. I'd like to be invited back."

God, that smile of his struck me dumb. It also made my heart race and my core throb. "It's not an imposition. We've enjoyed your company. And you're welcome back any time."

"You know, since I'm here," he paused. "I'm not sure what your plans are for dinner, but maybe I could take you ladies out to eat? It's not the home cooked meal I'd originally offered, which is still on the table, by the way, but if you haven't eaten and I haven't eaten...it's kind of a win-win."

"Oh mama, can we? My belly is so hungry." Maisie rubbed it to emphasize her point.

Wow, she was really putting it on tonight. It *was* nearly time for us to eat, and I didn't have anything special planned for dinner either. Not that I ever did. It was always whatever I could find in the fridge or the cabinets, which usually amounted to mac and cheese and chicken tenders. "Are you sure? I don't want to take you away from any plans you already made."

Pablo reached over Maisie's head and palmed my

cheek. My breath hitched in my chest at his touch, and I caught myself leaning into it.

"You're not taking me away from anything. I want to spend time with both of you. If I didn't want to take you out, I wouldn't have offered. So, how about we figure out where we want to go so this little munchkin doesn't starve to death?"

He pulled his hand away from my face and started tickling and growling at Maisie, who giggled and laughed. The two wrestled for a minute until Pablo picked her up and set her on her feet in front of him. Then he rose and placed his hand out, palm up. I let him help me up.

"I guess that's settled then. Let me just take Maisie to the bathroom first before we go. We'll be right back."

"Take your time."

"Come on, baby, let's get ready to go," I said.

She and I quickly did our business, and then we were back in the living room. Pablo remained patiently waiting. I picked up my bag from the floor near the door.

"I think we're ready."

"Excellent."

I held on to Maisie's hand and the three of us headed out into the hall. It was weird, yet nice having Pablo with us as we made our way down the stairs. He opened the door for us, and I stepped past him into the warmth of the sunny day still holding onto my daughter's hand.

"Do you have any idea where you'd like to go? Anything special you're hungry for?" he asked.

"Pasketti," Maisie sang out obviously already knowing what she wanted.

"Hmmm. Actually Italian does sound pretty good. I've kind of been..." my voice trailed off and my steps slowed, causing Maisie to glance up at me. She started to speak, but I shushed her, squeezing her hand. On the sidewalk next to a blacked out SUV stood River and a couple of guys I'd seen him talking to before. I tried not to be obvious, but I moved closer to Pablo and pulled Maisie into my side.

"What's wrong?" he asked, his voice low.

"It's him," I whispered out the side of my mouth.

Pablo went rigid next to me, but slowly relaxed, and I felt his fingers thread through mine. His touch comforted me a bit.

"Everything's going to be fine," he said in a low voice before raising it again to a normal pitch. "So, if my girls want spaghetti, Italian it is."

Then we were right next to the men. I couldn't stop myself. I caught River's gaze, but I quickly glanced away. The three of them stopped their conversation as we walked past. My whole body trembled and Maisie was quiet at my side.

Pablo, on the other hand, continued talking as though nothing unusual was going on. My fingers squeezed his hard, but he didn't even flinch. "There's either Bruna's or Franco's. They're not far from here. I've been to both and you can't go wrong with either one."

Maybe because of how calm he was, I was able to answer without a nervous catch to my voice. "We haven't been to Franco's in a while. Why don't we go there?"

"Baby girl, does Franco's sound good to you too?" Pablo tilted his head to look down at Maisie.

She nodded, the small movement surprising me. We moved further and further away from the men, but I was still acutely tuned in to any sound beside cars driving by, the kids playing basketball across the street, or our foot-steps on the sidewalk. There was nothing else though.

"I can already taste the breadsticks," I added, trying to let my body relax a bit. I loosened the death grip on Pablo's fingers.

"You and me both," he said.

Finally, we were no longer within hearing distance of River or his friends. I laid my head on Pablo's shoulder. "Thank you."

He gently squeezed my hand, rubbing his thumb against mine in a soothing gesture. "I told you everything would be fine."

I should have trusted him not to let anything happen to Maisie and me. She was still quiet, so I raised my head and looked down at her. "You okay, baby?"

"Yes, Mama. I not like that man."

"I know you don't, honey."

"Hey munchkin," Pablo addressed Maisie. "You don't have to worry about him. He's not going to bother you again."

"You promise?"

"Promise."

I sent him a sideways glance. There was such convic-tion behind that word. How could he be so sure?

He pulled his keys out of his pocket and the beep beep of a car lock disengaging came from the sedan a few feet in front of us. The headlights blinked twice with the sound. *Shit, the car seat.* I hadn't even thought about it. Seeing River had thrown me off.

"Everything alright?" Pablo asked at my hesitation.

"Yeah, I just forgot Maisie's car seat."

"I'm sorry. I didn't even think about it."

"Me either." I wasn't keen on heading back in the direction we just came. Not right now anyway.

"Do you have your keys? I'll run and get it."

"Are you sure?" I asked.

Pablo opened the back door and Maisie climbed in. He turned with his hand out. "Positive."

"Thank you."

I pointed out my car just in case he couldn't recall it, and within a few minutes, he was back. Once I got the car seat and Maisie situated, he opened my door for me as well and closed it behind me. Once he was at the wheel, he glanced into the backseat. "Hey, munchkin, you ready to pig out on some bread sticks and spaghetti?"

Hearing her giggle eased any remaining tension in my muscles from our brief encounter moments ago. "I'm ready."

"Then here we go."

We hadn't made it a block before Pablo reached over the console between us. Once again, he threaded his fingers through mine, and it wasn't just for show. The entire drive to the restaurant he continued holding my hand as though reassuring me that I had nothing to worry about. For the first time in five years, I actually began to believe that my life would be okay.

CHAPTER 17

THE RESTRAINT I'd displayed at seeing Oliver standing outside with those Los Lobos members would have made my family proud. Especially considering how scared Michele and Maisie had been and the danger he could have been putting her in. Not since the day outside the pool had Maisie been that quiet. Michele's fingers had been trembling when I'd slid mine through them. No doubt her daughter's had been as well. My hand had throbbed for several minutes from how tight she'd been gripping onto it.

I'd caught Oliver watching us, and I'd wanted to curse at him to not draw special attention to us. If shit went down with him and Los Lobos, and they thought he knew Michele or had a connection to her, they could try to use her as some sort of leverage. I swore to god, if that happened, the Captain would have to tear me away from him before I sent him to the hospital. Or worse.

Thankfully I'd kept my cool, which filtered over into

L.K. SHAW

Michele, who'd impressed me. She hadn't panicked, but rather played along with us being a happy family on our way to dinner. Except it hadn't felt like playing. It had felt all too right, in fact. The feel of her skin between my fingertips. The scent of her washing over me as she leaned in close and laid her head on my shoulder. It had done something to me. I wanted to see where this would lead.

"Dinner was delicious. Thank you so much," Michele said on our walk back to the car.

"You're welcome. I'm glad you enjoyed it. It's been too long since I've been to Franco's. I forgot how good their food is."

It had been a wonderful night. Maisie kept up most of the conversation, but I'd learned a few things about Michele, including how patient she was. Nothing seemed to ruffle her. She took everything in stride. I loved seeing the dynamic between the two of them. These two loved each other fiercely. And I wanted to be a part of that.

"I'm pretty sure I'm not going to need to eat the whole day tomorrow. I can't believe I stuffed my face like that. I'm a little embarrassed," she groaned once she settled into the passenger seat.

"No need to be. I ate twice as much as you. Then again, I do have all these muscles I need to feed." I mockingly flexed my bicep.

Michele covered her face and mumbled something behind her hands, while Maisie hooted in the backseat.

"You gots lots of muscles, Mister Pablo," she chimed in.

"See, even Maisie thinks so." I chuckled and nudged Michele's arm before tugging one of her hands off her face and holding it in mine. I couldn't stop touching her. She turned her head with a pout. "I'm never going to live that down."

"I promise I'll only bring it up when I need a boost to my self-confidence. It's nice knowing that you think of me in that way."

She didn't look convinced. Before long, we were back on her street, and I was finding a place to park. Oliver and his buddies were gone. Michele helped Maisie out of the car and the three of us walked to the apartment, stopping quickly to put the car seat back. This time, Maisie strolled between us.

My heart skipped at the sudden feel of tiny fingers clasping my hand.

Michele hesitated outside her door. Then she seemed to come to a decision, because she whirled and in a rush of breath started speaking. "Would you like to come in? I have to give Maisie a bath and read her a bedtime story, and it takes her forever to go to sleep, but if you want to hang out for a little bit, then you're welcome to come in. But only if you don't have something to do. Because if you do, I totally understand."

Man, this woman was adorable when she was nervous. And completely irresistible, without even knowing it.

"I can stay for a little while."

"Okay, great." Michele's expression tightened with nervousness again. "I don't have cable, but if you want you can turn the TV on. I'm hoping we won't be too long in the bathtub. If it gets too late and you have to leave, just holler."

I stepped forward and palmed her jaw. "I'm not in any rush. Take your time with your daughter. I'll still be here when you come out. I'm not going anywhere."

"Okay." She took Maisie's hand and the two of them disappeared down the hallway.

I settled on the couch, pulled out my phone, and started checking my emails.

Lots of splashing and giggles floated down the hallway, and I couldn't help but relish the sound. I'd been fascinated with babies after Ines' birth. She had been the happiest infant, never crying. She would bat her long lashes up at me whenever I'd peer over the edge of her crib, and I'd fallen head over heels in love with her.

I'd decided even at the age of six that I wanted to be a dad. If our father ever asked one of us to help, which was rare, I was the first one to volunteer. I'd fed her. Changed her diapers. Watched her grow up into this amazing woman who had a daughter of her own. I wanted that too.

Rapid footsteps, along with Michele calling her daughter's name, drew my attention over my shoulder just in time to see a pajama-clad Maisie rush down the hallway toward me. Her hair was wet and slicked back, and in her hand, yet another book.

"Mister Pablo, read me a bedtime story. Pretty please." She dove onto the couch next to me.

Michele hustled into view seconds later, her hair pulled up in a knot, cheeks flushed, and her shirt wet in places.

"You look like you wrestled with a wet monkey," I said with amusement.

She glanced down at herself with a shake of her head. "Somebody loves to see how high she can make the water splash if she slaps it."

"Can you blame her?" I looked down at the somebody

in question. "Who wouldn't want to know how high it goes, right?"

Maisie nodded in agreement, while Michele sighed with a grin on her lips. "Don't encourage her."

"Mama, Mister Pablo said he readed me a bedtime story," she announced.

Her mother crossed her arms and stared down with a steely glare at the munchkin currently getting my side wet. "Oh, he did, did he? Because all I heard was you telling him to read it to you."

"I askeded pretty please. I promise."

A little leery about getting between their discussion and possibly undermining Michele's authority and risking her anger, I cautiously added my support of Maisie. "She did ask pretty please."

Michele threw up her hands good-naturedly. "Man, I'm not going to win this one with you two am I? Alright, but only one story"—she emphasized with a single pointed finger—"young lady, and then it's time for bed."

"Okay." She handed me the book and curled up next to me, her wet head pressed against my arm. It was one of the best feelings ever.

Sandwiching her daughter between us, Michele took her place on the other side, tucked her feet up underneath her and propped her head on her arm against the back of the couch. I started to read. It wasn't long before the weight next to me became heavier as Maisie sagged against me, her eyes closed and her breathing soft. My voice grew quieter until I trailed off and gently shut the book. Neither her mother nor I spoke for a minute, waiting to see if she'd wake up, but she remained still.

"You're so good with her. She's never been like this

with anybody before. You must be some kind of toddler whisperer," Michele joked.

I shook my head. "Nah, I just think that kids can sense when people genuinely like them, and they respond to that. It's body language and how a person speaks to them. It sounds bad, but they're like dogs in that they can recognize friend or foe. I've always adored kids and Maisie can feel that vibe from me."

Michele was silent a moment longer, her gaze unfocused like she was elsewhere. Then she blinked and came back, but her expression was flat like her thoughts had been unpleasant. "That actually makes a lot of sense. I wish I had her same instinct about people. Anyway, I should probably get her laid down."

She rose slowly, trying not to disturb her daughter.

"Would you like me to take her?" I asked.

"No, that's okay. Thank you though. I'll just be a minute." Carefully, she picked up Maisie, whose eyes flickered open and drifted closed with a slight murmur and carried her down the hall. I waited patiently for a few minutes and then she was back.

"I probably should have asked you this an hour ago, but would you like something to drink? I don't have much to choose from though. Water, milk, or a juice box," she said with a small lift of her shoulder.

"Maybe some water." I wasn't really thirsty, but there was a new tension in her.

She wasn't the only one feeling a bit jittery. This was technically two dates for us, which meant she was only one date short of the longest dating spree I'd ever had.

"Here you go." She handed me the glass and our fingers brushed. A jolt hit me whenever we'd touched, but

I always managed to mask my reaction to her. But this time, it seared me, sending a spike of heat straight up my arm. I didn't hide my reaction. Instead, my gaze bore into Michele's, and I let her see exactly the effect she had on me.

CHAPTER 18

I COULDN'T REMEMBER BEING this nervous with a guy before. Not even with Warren when he'd first started paying attention to me. Back then, I'd been a naive, innocent child who had no idea the true consequences of, well, of anything. In the last five years I'd learned a lot. Including the need to be cautious.

The heat I'd hoped to see in Pablo's eyes was no longer hidden. An answering fever began to burn low in my belly, the sizzle spreading until my whole body was on fire.

"You're standing there like I'm going to grope you the minute you sit down."

I blinked and my gaze met Pablo's. He was staring up at me with a bemused expression. Flustered, I took a seat on the couch. "Sorry, I guess I'm just a little nervous."

He cocked his head at my confession. "You don't say?"

Against my will, a bubble of laughter popped out of me, and I sagged against the sofa back. "Is it that obvious?"

"Maybe a little. What are you nervous about?" He sounded genuinely curious.

My gaze hovered somewhere between Pablo's shoulder and his chin. "Everything, actually. I'm worried that I'm not good enough for you. That you're going to realize dating a woman with a kid isn't your thing. I worry you're going to break my heart. My daughter's heart. I'm worried that things right now are too perfect—that *you're* too perfect. I worry I'm going to close my eyes, and the moment I open them, reality is going to burst in and destroy the perfect world I feel like I've been living in for the first time in my life."

I felt both sick and relieved at the same time after blurting it all out like that. Pablo had that effect on me. It was like he wouldn't let me hide behind all my insecurities no matter how hard I tried. Afraid to see how he reacted to me word vomiting every single one of my feelings like that, I still didn't meet his eyes.

"That's a lot to be worried about. If you talk to Ines, she'll be happy to share with you all the ways I'm not perfect. Maybe that will make you feel better."

I huffed out a short bark of amusement at that. "It sounds so silly now that I've said it out loud."

"None of your feelings are silly," he said, scooting a little closer and lightly touching my arm. "I have a confession to make."

That had me meeting his gaze. "What's that?"

"I'm probably just as nervous as you are. For some of the same reasons."

What did Pablo have to be scared about? The man had everything. Looks, charm, kindness, a protective side that made me feel like I wasn't all alone. Best of all, Maisie seemed to love him. I couldn't figure out why he was still single. "You?"

"Yeah, me. I think about our age difference. You still have your whole life ahead of you, and I wonder why you would have any interest in a nearly crippled guy practically old enough to be your father. I also worry that I'm going to break your heart and Maisie's heart. Not intentionally, of course, but there's always a chance it could happen. That's a lot of pressure to make sure I get shit right."

My brain homed in on the fact that Pablo liked me. I focused so hard on that part of his speech that I nearly missed the rest of it. *Wait, huh?* "What in the world are you talking about? Old? Crippled? You have a small limp. That's not crippled. And you're not old enough to be my father."

"Okay, so maybe that's a little bit of a stretch. But see? It's okay to be worried about things. Talk to me about them, though. You don't have to handle them alone."

"This is what I mean about being too perfect." I gestured. "Most guys would think I was ridiculous. They'd blow off my concerns like they're nothing. Make me believe I'm imagining things. That I'm being silly."

Pablo reached out for my hands, holding them between us. "I don't know what kind of guys you dated in the past, but I'm not them. We all have insecurities. Mine happen to be my age and this stupid limp. The biggest thing we have to remember is to communicate with each other. To trust one another. Which is hard as shit. Especially if you've been hurt in the past. Which it sounds like you have."

"You have no idea."

"Who was it that hurt you?"

I shifted.

"His name was Jonas. I started dating him when Maisie was about eighteen months old. He wasn't the first guy I'd gone out with, but none of the others lasted more than a few dates. I was always upfront about having a daughter, as well as what I did for a living. Some acted like they were okay with it, while others immediately stopped calling. A few of them even met her, but then I think the reality of a kid really hit home and they weren't ready for that."

Looking back, I'd probably dodged a few bullets that way. But at the time all the rejections hurt.

"One day, we were at the grocery store, and I accidentally crashed into his shopping cart with mine. He struck up a conversation with me. Said hi to Maisie. He was all smiles—polite—and seemed to enjoy talking to me. He asked me for my phone number before we went our separate ways. I was pretty sure he wouldn't call, but the next day my phone rang. We talked forever and he asked me out on a date. Before long he and I were going out all the time. He brought me flowers and wrote me sweet romantic notes. Aside from that initial meeting at the store, he didn't spend time with Maisie. I wanted to make sure things would work out for longer than three or four dates before I let a guy meet her. I didn't want to confuse her."

I paused, reflecting on those few good months we'd had before it all went to shit. Pablo squeezed my hand. "That's perfectly understandable. I assume things went well and you introduced the two?"

Nodding, I continued. "Yes. About three months after our first date I thought we had hit the point in our relationship that I'd bring Maisie into it. And it was great for the first month or two. At least I thought it was. Until he started getting more and more impatient with her. She was two years old and testing her boundaries, which often led to her throwing a fit when she didn't get what she wanted. He was always yelling at her. Snapping at me for indulging in her tantrums. No was her favorite word. She loved saying it, but she sure didn't love hearing it. One day he got so angry when she wouldn't listen to him telling her she couldn't do something—I can't even remember what it was now—and he hit her."

My eyes burned. There were times I could still hear her screaming.

"I kicked him the hell out of my apartment and never saw him again. Maisie wasn't the same around people after that. She withdrew from strangers. Loud noises made her cry. Thank god that stopped, but she became this new, reserved little girl. I hated Jonas for so long. For turning my daughter into the scared version of herself." I took a deep breath. "And now, here you are. My daughter is a different person with you. That terrifies me, because I don't ever want to see her that way again if things don't work out between us."

"He was the one you didn't think liked your kid?"

I nodded.

"I stand by my previous statement. He's a fucking idiot."

"Thank you for that."

"You're welcome. Here's the thing. I can only make you one promise, and it's this. I will never intentionally do anything to hurt either one of you. God knows I'd never lay a hand on you or Maisie. You've met my family. Ines would murder me if I ever stepped out of line that way.

Estelle, Marguerite, and Landon would be right behind her, followed by my father and brothers. Brother-in-laws too. You'd be pulling each and every one's foot out of my ass."

I choked on the image he presented. He wasn't lying either. Brother or not, Ines would never tolerate Pablo hurting me or my daughter like that. Not that the thought of him physically hurting us ever crossed my mind.

"It's kind of weird actually talking like this. I don't mean that in a bad way. It's just..."

"Just what?" he encouraged after several seconds of silence.

My parents were the one topic I never discussed with anyone. Not any of the girls from *SINoritas*. Not even Ines. All she knew was they'd kicked me out of the house after I got pregnant.

"I'm not used to it," I said, finally. "My parents never talked to each other. Not unless they had to anyway. My mother spent all her time at the country club with her tennis instructor, who she was no doubt fucking, which is such a cliché. Meanwhile, my father spent all his time at his office, fucking his secretary. I'm pretty sure the only time they ever even saw each other was at the breakfast table every morning. They didn't even sleep in the same room."

"That must have been hard for you."

Was it? I always assumed that's what marriage was like. "I didn't really know any better. All the country club marriages I saw were the same way. Husbands and wives leading their own lives, barely speaking unless they were at one of those fancy charity events. Even then some of the men would flaunt their mistresses. It just seemed to be how things were done."

"And you were at a lot of these charity events?" Pablo asked.

"My fair share. At least in the two years before I was no longer welcome."

"So," he said with some hesitation. "You grew up wealthy?"

I laughed bitterly. "Yep. The whole silver spoon and everything. Shocking isn't it?"

"Didn't expect it, I'll admit."

"Yeah, it's not really something I like to talk about. Especially considering how far from it all I am now. And especially considering who my father is."

"You don't have to tell me anything you don't want to. Your past is yours. It doesn't have any bearing on who you are today. Not in my eyes anyway. I told you that. It's not a reflection of you."

"But it is. Like you said—my past made me who I am today. I'm coming to terms with it and realizing I'm doing okay."

"I think you're doing great. If my opinion matters at all."

"You may change your opinion once you find out who my father is."

Pablo's expression was questioning.

"Ralph Lewis."

Pablo blinked a few times and his head reared back, his expression quickly shifting from shock to anger. It nearly mirrored the look he'd worn when he arrived at my door earlier tonight.

"Your father is the Illinois Attorney General?"

I slowly nodded. "One and the same."

He didn't say anything for several minutes, but his entire body was rigid from his clenched jaw, the muscles in his cheeks dancing, to the fingers fisted at his side. "I can't believe it. I always respected him as a loving family man...holy, fucking shit. Do you mean to tell me that you're the teenage runaway daughter he's desperately been looking for these past four years? The one he's actually pleaded with, on national television, to come home or call and let them know you're okay?"

A snort escaped. "Is he still spouting that bullshit to people?"

"I think so. I mean, I haven't been paying a lot of attention lately, but it most definitely hasn't been that long since I saw him give a press conference."

"That sounds about right. Always looking for sympathy. I called my father after he gave his first one. I threatened to tell everyone the truth. He threatened to have me arrested."

Pablo sucked in a sharp breath.

"That was the last time I spoke to my parents until Maisie's first birthday. I don't know why I called. Maybe because I thought they'd changed. That maybe they missed me. Wanted to know how their granddaughter was doing. What a joke. I shouldn't have wasted my breath. I was still the awful daughter who could have ruined my father's public image and the family name."

"Jesus, Michele. I'm so sorry."

I waved off his sympathy. "I stopped worrying about my parents' approval a long time ago."

Pablo moved closer. He brushed the hair off my forehead, his eyes scanning my face before settling to meet my gaze. "For what it's worth, I think you're the one who's better off without him. Any father would be proud to call you his daughter. To call Maisie his granddaughter. By not having you in his life, he's the one losing out."

Ever so slowly he leaned forward, his eyes still laser-focused on me. My eyelids fluttered closed the moment Pablo pressed his mouth to mine. A soft brush across my skin. Once. Twice. On the third pass, the kiss deepened. His lips were gentle. Cautious. Too cautious. I opened my mouth the tiniest bit, and it was all the incentive he needed. His fingers speared my hair, clasping my head in a possessive move that made me gasp. He took full advantage and plundered it with his tongue.

The taste of wine, mixed with the after-dinner mint he'd had, burst across my tastebuds. It was a heady flavor. The kiss went on and on. His free hand didn't linger in one place too long, but skated across my cheek, down my neck and shoulders. It traveled the length of my arm, then slid to my waist before finally resting on my hip. It was a comforting embrace.

Pablo didn't try to press for more than the soul-shaking kiss, which only made me yearn for him to. I shifted to my knees and pressed my body forward until we were chest to chest, and I wrapped my arms around his neck, taking the initiative to deepen the kiss further. I sensed he was holding back. Letting me lead. It only fanned the fire from the embers that had been waiting to flare back to life with just his touch.

I tilted my head to get a better angle, and I moved my leg until I was straddling his lap. Scorching heat raced through my core at his erection pressing exactly where I needed. My hips swiveled trying to generate the right amount of friction. A moan slipped from my lips to his. A kiss had never seared me like this one.

Pablo's lips were like magic. He knew just how to tease me to make me want more. And did I ever want more. At long last I slid my fingers through his beautiful hair. It was just as soft as I'd imagine. I tangled my fingers in his dark waves and held him tightly to me, pressing my body harder against his erection. I couldn't get close enough.

His strong hands clutched at my hips, guiding my movements to increase the friction between my legs. I should have been embarrassed that I was dry humping Pablo in the middle of my living room. Instead, I prayed Maisie didn't come out of our room so I didn't have to stop. I was chasing that soaring feeling that followed behind the tension building inside me. It was tightening further with each thrust of my pelvis against his.

His tongue lashed mine, and the hold on my hips tightened. I ground myself harder and faster against Pablo. The throbbing in my core spread until ecstasy hit and then exploded. My body pulsed and shuddered with my release. I collapsed in a limp, weakened heap, forehead resting on his, our chests rapidly rising and falling as though we'd run a mile.

"Wow," I breathed out. "That was..."

"Yeah it was," Pablo agreed.

I giggled, sitting back on my heels, my butt resting on his thighs, not quite ready to lose our connection despite the heat spreading up my neck and cheeks. I pushed back the shyness creeping in and stared down at the man whose eyes glowed with arousal.

"Do you want me to…" My voice trailed off and my eyes drifted downward.

Pablo's gaze followed mine. "No. You don't need to. That was for you."

"Are you sure?"

"I'm positive. This wasn't about quid pro quo. I'm glad you enjoyed yourself."

"I should say thank you."

He sent me a quizzical look, one brow raised.

"Oh my god." I playfully smacked his chest. "Not for that. I just meant thank you for not judging me. You never once blamed me for what happened between my parents and me. That's part of the reason why I haven't told anyone. The last person I told thought I was in the wrong and should go crawling back to my parents and ask for forgiveness."

"I'm not going to ask who that was, because I can already guess."

I slid off his lap onto the couch next to him and took a page from Maisie's book, cuddling up against his side. My fingers played with the button on his polo.

"I had a really nice time tonight." It hit me what I just said. "I mean dinner and spending time with you. Not just, um, you know."

"I did too." There was amusement in his voice.

The ringing of his phone startled me.

"Sorry, I should get this," he said, leaning sideways to pull his phone out of his back pocket. "Rodriguez."

Pablo jerked upright.

"Si." He rose from the couch and paced while he listened to whoever was on the other end speak. "Claro, puedo ir. Estoy en veinte minutos."

He tapped the screen on his phone and pocketed it

before turning to me. "I'm sorry. That was work. Something came up and I have to go."

I moved to stand next to him. "I understand. Be careful."

"I'll call you tomorrow." He gave me a quick kiss and was out the door before I could even say goodbye.

CHAPTER 19

I RUSHED OUT of Michele's apartment. I reached the stairs, and a door opened. Oliver and I both stopped in surprise, his eyes widening for a moment before his expression blanked. He turned around and went back inside. I'd see him again shortly. In less than twenty minutes, I was at my desk at the precinct.

Shortly after, Oliver came striding through the room, Except he wasn't alone. The Captain was leading him in. My boss took a seat across from me and Oliver pulled over a chair from the neighboring desk, flipped it backwards, and straddled it.

"What's going on?" I asked.

"I'm pretty sure Morales killed Salazar," Oliver replied.

Shit. We already knew that was a possibility, but to hear it confirmed…"What makes you think that?"

He rubbed the back of his neck and didn't quite meet my eyes. "Earlier tonight, I was talking to a couple of the guys I've made friends with inside Los Lobos. They mentioned a meeting last night between Morales and some *high-powered chica*. After it was over and she'd left, he and his close circle of enforcers started celebrating. Talking about how things are going to change for the better for them. How he got rid of someone standing in their way of more money and power. There's been a rumor going around that Salazar hasn't been seen for a few days. Could be a coincidence. Or it might not be."

I glanced between Oliver and Cap, who'd remained silent this whole time. "So what's the next step?"

"As of right now? Nothing. Garrison is going to continue with his original assignment, bringing down Morales and Los Lobos on narcotics charges. We're letting homicide deal with the possible murder investigation. That's not our objective. Arresting drug dealers and getting that shit off the streets is."

From the look in Oliver's eyes, he wasn't satisfied with that. It was an expression familiar to me.

"Rodriguez, I want you to continue in your role as Garrison's contact. Nothing changes in that aspect. We're going to keep building our case against Los Lobos. Once we can get some solid evidence on the next deal happening, we'll take them down. Continue getting the little fish to flip on the bigger ones until finally we have the shark in our sites. Or in this case, the alpha wolf."

For a second I was tempted to ask to be removed from the case. I was still pissed at Oliver, but I could already hear the Captain's response. *Keep your personal shit out of your work shit*. All he cared about was making arrests.

"What happens if homicide gets enough evidence on Morales and they charge him?" I asked.

"Have you been in touch with your contact in the DEA?"

I nodded. My relationship with Landon was a sore spot with the Captain. With Landon pushing for more inter-agency cohesion, we'd made a significant more number of arrests with shared intel. It was only because of her that we got credit for the King bust.

"Reach out to her again," he said. "See if she has heard anything about Salazar being hit. It's possible we might be able to get Morales to flip on Señora Valesquez if it means taking a plea for a lesser charge. But they have to have enough evidence to charge him in the first place."

"I'll call her first thing in the morning, and let you know as soon as I find anything out," I told him.

Cap rose from his chair. "I'm going home. You two catch up on any pertinent news that needs shared."

I waited for him to leave before picking up my keys from my desk.

"So you're the boyfriend."

My body tensed, and I glared at him. "I don't think it's a good idea for you to bring her up."

He showed me his palms. "I'm not trying to start anything."

I studied him and read the sincerity in his expression. "We aren't there yet, but it's heading in that direction."

"That's good, man. I've known you for years. This is the first time you seem to be really happy. I'm glad. You deserve a nice girl like her."

Who was this person in front of me? This wasn't the Oliver Garrison I knew. "Thanks," I said with a small amount of suspicion.

"Nah, really. I mean it. I saw the three of you together tonight. Thanks for not ratting me out to the Captain, by the way," he said with a sheepish grin. "Anyway. I saw you with her and that little girl of hers. You guys looked like a real family. It was nice seeing you like that. I hope you told her I was sorry for being such an asshole."

"I didn't tell her who you were. Despite the fact that I wanted to murder you, and although I trust her, I'm not going to blow your cover. I made sure they knew that you wouldn't bother either of them again though."

"I appreciate that. And I really am sorry."

"I'm still pissed at you though," I said without heat.

He only nodded. "I don't blame you. I would be, too, if she was my girl."

Not wanting to talk about Michele with him anymore I rose. "Give me a call if you hear anything more, will ya?"

"Sure thing."

I left him sitting there. A quick glance at my watch told me it was late. Too late to call Michele. I didn't want to wake either her or Maisie. Instead, I headed home. To my surprise, Brody and Ines were there.

"Hey," I greeted them. "What are you guys doing here?"

Ines pecked my cheek. "We had dinner with Papá. Where have you been all night?"

I settled on the love seat. "Just got done meeting with Oliver and the Captain. Looks like we might have a situation with Salazar."

This had everyone's attention.

"Salazar?" Brody repeated.

"Yes, but I don't have confirmation of anything yet. I actually need to talk to Landon tomorrow. There's a rumor he's dead and that Maria Luis Valesquez is behind it."

"Holy shit," Ines breathed out. "Are you serious? What does that mean if it's true?"

"No idea," I said. "No one seems to know what her intentions are. I was hoping Landon could shed some light. You have any thoughts, Brody? I know you were out of the game by the time Valesquez showed up. But did you hear any rumors about her while you worked for Álvarez?"

"Not really. I only ever dealt with Raúl Escobar. He mentioned something a time or two about how he couldn't believe she was trying to become a part of their world, but that's about it."

Ines snorted. "I guess that's what he gets for underestimating a woman. Especially since she was the one who apparently killed him. Bet that came as a shock."

We all stared at her and she sent back an innocent expression. "What?"

Leave it to my sister to admire a murderous businesswoman moving up the corporate ladder of drug smuggling.

"Anyway, so basically all we know about her is that she hated Salazar and wanted to destroy everything he worked for. We know she has gained a lot of powerful allies. And she's not afraid to murder people who stand in her way. We just don't know in the way of what."

CHAPTER 20

IT HAD BEEN two days since Pablo had rushed out of my apartment. Two days since that amazing night. Two days since I'd felt his lips on mine. I was anxious for it to happen again. And again. My belly was flip flopping with anticipation at the thought of spending another evening with him. I pulled in front of his lovely two-story home. It was sweet that he lived with his father. It showed how close of a family they were. It also made me yearn for that sense of closeness.

"Come on, baby, let's go see what Mister Pablo is fixing us for dinner," I said, getting Maisie out of her car seat.

"Yay. My tummy is so hungry. And I missed him. Do you think he missed me too?"

It made me so happy to see how much my daughter liked Pablo, but it also worried me. "I'm sure he did."

"Can I climb again, Mama?"

"We'll see, but not before we eat." We reached the front door, and I rang the bell, jitters still hitting me.

The door opened, and there he was, looking devastatingly gorgeous like always.

"Hi," he greeted us warmly and stepped back to let us in. "Come on in."

We stepped inside and he closed us in. Then he turned and dropped to a knee in front of Maisie who practically leapt into his arms and gave him a huge hug.

"Well that was some hello. Thank you," he said, hugging her in return.

"I misseded you," she pouted.

"I missed you too, munchkin." He rose to his feet and then I was in his arms next. "I missed you as well."

"Me too," I whispered back.

Pablo dropped a brief kiss on my lips which made Maisie giggle. Despite his warm greeting, he seemed a bit more tense than usual. We hadn't discussed why he'd had to rush out the other night, but after the things he'd said on our coffee date, I guessed he was struggling with something. I didn't want to push for him to tell me, because he probably couldn't tell me.

"I hope you two brought your appetite, because I might have made far too much food." He led us out of the den and into the kitchen. "Why don't you have a seat? I'm just finishing up and then everything should be ready. I hope you don't mind, but my father might pop in to say hello."

"Of course I don't mind. I like Ernesto very much. It's always nice to see him."

"That's so lovely to hear. It's always a pleasure to see you lovely ladies," a voice came from the doorway.

I pivoted to see the man in question standing there with a broad smile on his tanned and weathered face.

There was such a strong resemblance between father and son, no one would doubt them being related.

"Thank you, Ernesto."

He moved into the room and stopped next to Maisie. "How are you today, pequeño mono?"

Maisie giggled. "You sound funny."

Ernesto drew back in mock offense. "What? You don't like being called a little monkey? Maybe I can teach you Spanish the next time you come for a visit."

"What is Spanish?"

"It is the language of my ancestors. You speak English, and I speak English and Spanish," he explained.

She turned to me, her eyes wide with excitement. "Mama, Mister 'nesto taught me 'panish."

"Wow, that's very exciting. You're going to be the smartest girl I know."

"Well, I won't bother you anymore. I merely wanted to come in and say hello. Pablo has been working hard on this meal to impress you."

"Jesus, Dad." A flush dusted his cheeks, and I couldn't stop my snicker. The good-natured ribbing this family did to each other always made me laugh.

Ernesto kissed me on the cheek, winked, and then disappeared back through the doorway and down the hall. I finally took a seat after helping Maisie up in her chair, where someone had kindly placed a booster seat. One I'm guessing had belonged to Pablo's niece or nephew at some point.

"Thirty-four years and I don't think my father will ever get tired of embarrassing his children," he said from his position in front of the stove. I would have offered to set the table, but it was already done.

"I think it's sweet." I glanced around. "Is there anything I can do to help? I feel bad just sitting here while you work."

"You're good. In fact," he paused before pivoting with the pot held between two hands. "The food is ready."

For the next forty minutes we ate and laughed while Maisie and Pablo chatted about everything under the sun. She regaled him with stories of what she'd done at preschool today and sang him a song she'd learned in music class. She spelled her name for him several times and per her request, he taught her how to spell his name. It was everything I imagined a normal family would do any night of the week.

"What about you?" he addressed me. "Do you have any special talents? Maisie showed off her beautiful singing voice. I'm sure she got that from you."

I nearly bowled over from laughter. "I promise you, she did not get her singing voice from me. I could curdle milk. I'm afraid I wasn't gifted with any special talents."

"That's not true. You have a talent for making people smile."

"I think that is the nicest thing anyone has ever said about me."

"It's the absolute truth." He leaned across the table for another brief kiss.

"You keep kissing me like that and I'm going to get used to it."

"Good, I hope so."

We rose from the table, clearing it off, and began to clean up. Maisie pitched in, and I let her help me load the dishwasher. The minute we finished, she was bouncing excitedly. "Can I go climb now, Mama? Pretty please?"

"If Mister Pablo doesn't mind."

He gestured toward the door. "Lead the way."

It was a beautiful evening, and we made our way across the backyard toward the jungle gym. I parked myself in one of the swings while Maisie began her trek up the rock climbing wall. Just like the last time, Pablo stood at the bottom waiting for her to jump in his arms once she reached the top.

"Catch me, papa," she hollered out before going airborne. Pablo froze for a moment but managed to wrap his arms around her before she tumbled to the ground. His eyes flashed to mine, and I hustled over, closing the distance between us.

He set Maisie on her feet and then lowered himself to her level. "Hey, munchkin, you know I like you bunches, right?"

Her eyes darted between the two of us before landing back on Pablo with uncertainty. She nodded slowly. His throat bobbed and he seemed to be measuring what he said. I wanted to jump in, but I didn't even know what to say about our current situation. I should have expected this to happen, but somehow I didn't.

"I like your mama too. But you know I'm not your papá, right?"

"I want you to be my papa." Her voice was soft. "Zoey has a papa. 'tina and Nich'las has a papa. Why can't you be my papa?"

Finally, I managed to find some words. I squatted down next to the two of them. "It doesn't work that way, baby. Mister Pablo and I like to spend time together and we like to spend time with you, but a mama and papa usually get married first. Not all the time, but lots of times."

"Why don't you be married then?" She said it as though it was the most logical thing in the world.

"When people get married," Pablo said. "It's because they love each other and want to spend the rest of their lives together. But they have to spend lots of time together first so they can fall in love. It doesn't always happen, although they hope it does."

Again her eyes tracked between us. "We spended lots of time together."

He nodded. "We have. And if your mama and I are lucky, we'll keep spending time together. With you too. But for now, how about we stick with Pablo, okay?"

Maisie had that mulish expression she always got when she wasn't getting her way. I held my breath, waiting for the tantrum to strike. She didn't often have them, but everyone once in a while, she'd get really upset about something, usually random, and have a meltdown. Until this moment. A miracle happened and she took in a shuddering breath. "Okay," she said.

Pablo hugged her tight. "That's my girl."

Disaster averted, but a new tension rose between him and I. A giant blob of awkwardness hung heavy between us. I hated it and wanted it to go away. Maisie and he went back to playing their game of climb and catch, but it didn't have the same levity and fun that it did before. At least not for me.

"Mama, will you push me, please?" She asked after her countless time of reaching the ground. Apparently, she was bored with the rock wall and ready to move on.

"Of course, honey."

Maisie climbed up into the swing and I slowly pushed her until that too grew tiresome for her.

"We should probably head into the house," Pablo suggested.

"Yeah, she's getting tired."

Ernesto greeted us inside the kitchen. "Did you have fun out there?"

"I climbeded and climbeded the wall and mama pushed me in the swing and Pablo says I should call him Pablo and not papa, even though I want him to be my papa."

She wasn't going to let it go. Luckily, Pablo's father took it all in stride. "My goodness that's quite an adventure you had tonight. You know that calling someone papá is something you need to think very hard about? It's nice that you like him that much, but you have to remember that you don't want just anyone to be your papá. They must earn that title. They have to promise to always be there for you. Protect you. Love you. It's an honor to be chosen, but you must make sure you choose right. Take your time before deciding. Can you do that?"

Maisie stared up at Ernesto. The expression on her face was one of intent concentration as though she was taking very seriously what he was saying to her.

"Yes, sir," she said.

"Good," he nodded. "If it's okay with your mama, I found a book you might like. It used to be Cristina's, and it was one of her favorites. I'd be happy to read it to you if you want."

She turned her gaze up to me. "Can I, Mama?"

"Sure, baby, since Mister Ernesto offered."

He held his hand out to her, and she trustingly placed

her small one inside his much larger one and the two of them strolled out of the kitchen and into the den leaving Pablo and I alone. Ernesto seated himself in his recliner and Maisie climbed up into his lap. Before long the two were intent on the story.

I pivoted nervously in Pablo's direction, not sure how to address everything that happened this evening. His gaze was on his father and my daughter and there was such a look of longing in his eyes that it actually took my breath away. He blinked and met my gaze. His smile was one of self-consciousness.

"Not exactly how I expected this evening to turn into," he said.

"You and me both. I'm sor—"

Pablo's finger covered my lips. "No apologies, remember?"

He lowered his hand, and I nodded. "No apologies."

"Come on, let's sit." With a hand to my lower back he guided me to the table. "I hope you enjoyed dinner."

So we weren't going to talk about what happened outside then. My emotions volleyed between relief and annoyance. "It was delicious. I think you're a better cook than you give yourself credit for."

"It helps when you have a father who spends all his free time in here. You pick up a few things over the years. He's teaching Brody how to cook for Ines."

That didn't surprise me in the least. "I'm sure she's loving that."

"Anything that will get her out of cooking a meal she'll take. Whatever it is. That is one thing she is terrible at. She tried making a few recipes for us growing up and they all turned into a complete disaster." Pablo shuddered as though remembering some of those terrible meals.

"I don't dare laugh, because I'm probably on her level when it comes to skills in the kitchen. I'd never even turned on a stove before in my life until I started volunteering at the women's shelter where I lived after Maisie was first born. I forgot to turn it off and nearly started the kitchen on fire. After that, the women all kept a close eye on me whenever it was my turn to help cook." I remembered those days fondly, even though they were some of the toughest of my life.

A lull flowed between us. I debated on bringing up what happened earlier, but decided against it. The silence continued until finally Pablo broke it.

"Will you tell me about Maisie's dad?"

I snorted. "She doesn't have a dad. She has a sperm donor. Honestly, though, it's just one of those sad stories of a girl who thought some boy loved her."

He laid his hand on mine. "I'd still like to hear it, if that's okay. If it's too painful, though, I understand."

Painful had been four years ago. Over time, the pain has faded to a dull throb that occasionally flared back to life during certain times. Mostly when I saw other kids with their dads at the park or doing things together, Maisie's birthday, and on days when I was so fucking tired and wished that I had someone to help with dinners and bath times. To just take all the pressure off of me for being…everything and everyone to my daughter.

"Warren was two years older than me. I was the shy, nerdy, awkward fourteen-year-old who loved books. Always had one with me, everywhere I went. One day I saw him outside playing tennis. I recognized him from school, of course." I paused remembering that first time. "Suddenly, I didn't have any interest in whatever it was I was reading. All I could do was watch him out there. It became my ritual. I'd run to my spot at the window, and I wouldn't move until he left the court."

My fingers twisted around each other on top of the table. A nervous habit I'd picked up as a kid and hadn't quite gotten rid of.

"One day, I found him sitting in my chair. He told me he wanted to meet the person always watching him. I'd been mortified. I had no idea he'd been able to see me. Embarrassed, I took off running. He chased me down and apologized. Then he started talking to me. Asked me questions like he wanted to get to know me. I fell head over heels."

"You don't have to say anymore," Pablo said.

"No, I just need to get it out. I've been holding onto this for so long. It actually feels good to get it out of my system."

He covered my hand with his. "If you're sure."

I nodded. "He never talked to me at school, but I just chalked it up to the fact that we were in different grades and we didn't see each other much. But anytime we were together at the tennis courts, we'd sneak off by ourselves. At first it was innocent. We'd talk about all the things we had in common. Then one day, he kissed me. Over the next year things progressed...beyond kissing."

"He didn't—?" Pablo ground out.

"No. Sure there was probably a little extra coercion with the whole 'if you loved me, you'd let me', but no, he never forced me."

He growled low in his throat as though he didn't quite believe that. Looking back, I wasn't sure I did either.

"After I found out I was pregnant, my parents were horrified. They demanded to know who the father was, so I told them. Of course, when they confronted Warren and his parents, he lied. He lied about all the time we spent together. He lied about all the stories we'd shared. He lied about everything."

"That's why you don't like liars," Pablo whispered as though talking to himself.

"Yes. He's the reason why. My parents believed him." My gaze grew unfocused as I recalled that last day in their house. I blinked to clear it.

I grew uncomfortable with this vulnerability I'd just exposed. I shifted in my chair and glanced at the clock hanging on the wall. "Gosh, it's getting late. We should probably get going. I still need to give Maisie a bath before bedtime. And you know how that goes."

Pablo's gaze bored into me. I just wanted to go home.

"Okay," he said.

We both rose from the table, and he followed me into the den. Both Ernesto and my little girl were asleep, her head resting on his chest, the book lying closed on his lap. My heart pinched with a bittersweet pain. This was what my dad was missing out on, and it was his own fault.

Pablo's father acted more like a grandfather than her biological one. The more time I spent with this family, the further I fell in love with them. The man at my side was no exception. I didn't want to call it love. We were barely getting to know each other. To scratch the surface of this possible relationship.

I'd never wanted anything more in my life though. I

wanted Pablo. I wanted what Ines and Brody had. What Victor and Estelle had. I wanted to become a part of this family so badly I nearly physically ached with the need. A warm touch brushed across my hand, and Pablo's fingers threaded through mine. I glanced up at him. Did my expression match his? The one of longing and hope?

"They look like they belong together, don't they?" He asked softly.

"Very much so."

Pablo didn't say anything else, only nodded. He brushed a kiss across my forehead and then gently shook his father's shoulder. "Papá. Michele and Maisie are heading home."

Ernesto mumbled and blinked his eyes before drowsily opening them fully and looking down at the little girl still asleep on his lap. "Goodness that didn't take her long."

"You either, apparently," Pablo joked before reaching down and scooping Maisie up in his arms. Her lids didn't even flutter. Her head merely settled on his shoulder, still fast asleep.

Together we walked out to my car where he gently laid her in her car seat before turning to me and pulling me against his chest. "Call me when you get home so I know you made it safely."

My hands splayed across his chest, and I nodded. "I will. I'll check my calendar about Thursday too."

"Good." He paused a moment, his gaze flittering over my face. "We should also talk later about what happened earlier tonight."

I sighed. "Yeah, you're probably right."

With a finger below my chin, he tipped my head up so

we were looking at each other. "Everything's good. We're good. Better than good, in fact."

Pablo lowered his head and sealed our mouths together, flicking his tongue along the seam, coaxing me to open for him. He dipped inside and teased me for several minutes before pulling back. His arms tightened around me, warming me, and then he released his hold. "Don't forget to call."

"I won't," I said, getting in the driver's seat. He closed the door behind me, and then I was on my way home, reliving that kiss, as well as dreading the conversation we definitely needed to have soon.

CHAPTER 21

I KNOCKED on Michele's door with a sweaty-palmed fist. Before long the chain jingled and the deadbolt clicked. This was it. I drank in the sight of her. No matter how many times we were together, each time I saw her she pulled me further under her spell. The funny thing was, she didn't even try. She had no idea the effect she had on me.

"Hi." No doubt a silly grin spread across my face.

"Hi," she greeted me. "Come on in. We're just about ready."

She closed us inside and then moved past. "We had a minor accident, so if you want to have a seat, we'll be right out."

"Take your time."

I settled on the couch while Michele disappeared down the hallway. I took her comment about a minor accident to mean something with Maisie. Which could be anything from bathroom accident to spilling something on her clothes and having to change. I wasn't in any hurry to leave. In fact, sitting here gave me a chance to calm my nerves. In no time at all, the two of them came from down the hall.

"Mister Pablo," Maisie yelled at seeing me. She raced around to my side of the couch and jumped on me, nearly kneeing me in the balls in the process. I barely managed to shift so I got nailed in my hip. It didn't help that it was my left leg. I bit back a groan as her bony knee dug into my thigh. Still, the feel of her arms squeezing me in a tight hug more than made up for it.

"Hey, baby girl," I managed to say. "Are you ready for the festival? I hope you're bringing an empty tummy, because there's going to be lots of food to eat."

She pulled away and worried her lip, her gaze not meeting mine. "I already emptied my tummy on accident."

I wasn't sure how to take that. "That's okay. Accidents happen. I hope you're feeling better."

Maisie's eyes met mine and she nodded emphatically. "Oh, yes, all better now."

"Good. Are you ready to go then? I think there might even be some fun rides we can try."

That put a sparkle of excitement in her baby blues. "Yay, I love rides."

Michele, standing at the end of the sofa, laughed at that, finally adding to our conversation. "How do you know you love rides? We've never been on any."

Maisie slid off my lap, stood as tall as her short body would go, and put her hands on her hips. "I just know."

I couldn't stop the burst of laughter. "Well, I guess we'll just have to take your word for it."

Pushing up from the couch, I rose to my feet and then

held out my hand. Michele laid her fingers in my palm and I pulled her in for a hug. She felt too good in my arms not to. I loved how she molded against me and fit perfectly under my chin.

"I should have done this when I walked through the door," I said against her hair.

Next to us, Maisie giggled.

"Better late than never," she replied, her arms tightening the slightest bit. Reluctantly I pulled back. Michele's cheeks were a pale pink.

"Alright, are you two lovely ladies ready to go have some fun?"

Maisie whooped and jumped around. After we locked up the apartment, the three of us headed outside. We stopped at Michele's car, remembering to get the car seat this time, and transferred it into mine. Once Maisie was settled in, we were off.

"Tell me more about this festival we're going to. It sounds interesting. I'm all about discovering new foods."

"It's the Fiesta del Sol. They hold it every summer and have for the last forty-some years, I think. It's in Pilsen, and just so happens to be the largest Latino festival in the Midwest. It's probably been twenty-five years since I've ventured down there. My parents used to bring us all the time when we were kids, and we always had a good time. I'm sure it's changed a lot since I was last here though."

"Maisie has been talking about it nearly non-stop since I told her you were taking us. We've never been to anything like it before. Not unless you count a small 4-H fair we went to up in Waukegan. But that was for the animals. She was going through the phase where she was learning about farm animals and loved every single one of them. One weekend we drove up there so she could see the cow, pigs, chickens, and goats. I think there were some horses as well. She lasted all of an hour before she became exhausted from the excitement, which then made her cranky. So we left. Hopefully she'll last longer than that today."

"If she doesn't, then it's okay. We'll have fun for however long we're there. Isn't that right, Maisie?"

"I'm gonna ride all the rides. Mama said I can eat as much food as I want because it won't spoil my supper cause I'm gonna eat everything."

Michele's laughter followed mine. "Well, don't eat so much you get a tummy ache."

Traffic thickened the closer to the festival we got, but I eventually found a lot that had a couple open spaces left. I paid the attendant and we started the short trek to where the first street had been closed off and a row of food carts began.

With Maisie between us, we each held her hands. She started swinging her arms forward and backward, so Michele and I ramped up the momentum and soon Maisie was swinging between us, landing with a stomp and a giggle.

The scent of cooking wafted all around us. We stopped at a couple of the food trucks for some samples before continuing to wander around. There were tents lining both sides of the street full of tables covered with various craft items representing a vast array of Latinx and Hispanic culture. Bright colors popped everywhere we turned. It was a beautiful sight.

"Oh, Mama, look at this pretty dolly." Maisie tugged us over to a tent with a display of dolls wearing what looked like hand sewn dresses. She turned her bright blue eyes up to her mother. "Can I get her? Pretty please?"

"Sweetie, we just got here. Maybe there will be something else you'll find that you'll like better," Michele said.

Before I could blink, those same eyes were peering up at me, pleading with a wet shimmer. "Mister Pablo. Please can I have the dolly? I promise I'll be a good girl."

Shit.

"Maisie Danielle," Michele scolded.

I was so out of my element here. Ines would be laughing at me, because no doubt there was a panicked expression on my face while I tried to navigate the current situation. "Munchkin, I'm sorry, but your mama said you need to wait. See if you find something you like better. You never know, you might find this super cool puzzle or maybe some books. I know you like those. Why don't we keep looking. If you can't find anything else, maybe we can come back here."

God, not the crying. Maisie's bright blue eyes sparkled with wetness as tears spilled over and raced down her cheeks. Next came the lower lip trembling. "Pretty, pretty please?"

The tears kept coming, streaming. I frantically looked at Michele for some help. Thankfully she took over, because I had no idea how to handle this situation. She bent down and gently clasped Maisie's hand in one of hers while wiping the tears away with the other.

"You know we've talked about asking for things and when I say no or let's wait and think about it. Do you remember that?" she asked softly.

Tears still flowed, but they were slowing. Maisie nodded. "Yes, Mama."

"I didn't tell you you couldn't have it, but we have to make sure that the thing we pick is what we really want. It's something big girls have to learn. And I know you're a big girl."

Michele pulled her daughter in for a hug and the two tightly wrapped their arms around each other. They separated and the rest of the tears were wiped away and Michele kissed Maisie's nose. "I love you."

"I love you too, Mama."

Thank god that crisis had been averted. It only emphasized how unprepared I was for this.

"Are we ready to keep looking around?" I asked tentatively.

"We're ready."

Maisie was much more subdued once we began walking again, but finally she returned to her laughing pleasant self. She continued admiring things, but she still didn't pick anything else that she liked. We rode a few rides including the Ferris wheel and the tea cups, which made me nauseated from the spinning. By the time we got off the short ride, I worried I might toss up the food we'd sampled earlier.

Soon Maisie grew tired, her steps slowing. I picked her up and carried her on my hip. She laid her head on my shoulder in the most trusting manner. It hit me straight in my heart. We made our way back through the festival and the craft section. There, on the table, was the doll that Maisie had desperately wanted. I glanced at Michele and then my gaze shifted over to the tent nearest us. She gave a short nod, and I walked with Maisie over there.

Within moments, we were heading back to the car with a new doll as part of our entourage. I opened the door for

Michele and placed a drowsy little girl in the car seat before getting behind the wheel. A glance in the rearview mirror showed Maisie's eyes falling closed, her arms clutching the dolly tightly to her chest. My fingers found Michele's as I carefully made my way down the busy streets.

"I didn't fuc—fudge things up too bad back there, did I?" I asked softly, not wanting to disturb the sleeping girl in the back.

Michele's lips tipped up on one side. "You did fine. We're still learning that we can't have the first thing we see every single time. Most of the time she gets it, but I think you were treated to a special show today. There are times she tests boundaries, and I guess she figured the tears would cajole you into letting her have what she wanted. I don't know how many guys would have handled it as well as you did."

"Really? Because I was floundering."

She squeezed my fingers. "You didn't yell at her for crying and you didn't let her manipulate you with her tears. I think you did more than fine."

"Thank god."

We drove in silence for a few blocks.

"I hope you enjoyed the festival," I said.

"It was wonderful. The food was out of this world. I swear if I keep hanging out with you, I'm going to be spoiled with all the delicious meals I keep getting."

"You deserve to be spoiled. You both do. And I'm more than happy being the one doing the spoiling." There was nothing I wanted more, in fact. I was falling head over heels for this woman and her daughter. Hearing Maisie call me papa had been the best thing I'd ever heard. I wanted to hear it again and again. Every day. No matter how fucking scary it was.

Perhaps because of the late hour, I had trouble finding a place to park that wasn't too far from Michele's building. I drove around for over five minutes before finally a spot two blocks away opened up. We exited the car, and I scooped the sleeping girl up. With her in one arm, I reached down and laced my fingers through Michele's, connecting the three of us together.

The closer we got to the apartment building, the louder the raucous laughter and music got. A group of people loitered out front. From this distance I couldn't discern if any of them were Oliver or not. The bright lights of an approaching vehicle momentarily blinded me. I squinted and jerked my head to the side. Then a sound I still heard in my dreams on occasion blasted through the night.

Rapid-fire gunshots exploded from the passing SUV. Screams pierced the night air.

"Get down! Get down!" I yelled, pushing Michele to the ground on the passenger side of a car parked along the curb. I dove next to her, as bullets continued to fly, trying to be careful with the delicate package in my arms whose screams joined everyone else's. I tugged both Maisie and Michele tightly to my chest, draping as much of my body over theirs as I could, trying to protect them. Both were crying and wails of pain, fear, and sorrow echoed around us as the last sounds of gunfire faded. Tires squealed and the SUV took off down the street.

"Are you guys okay? Are you hit? Michele, talk to me." I ran my hands and gaze over them, trying to make sure that I didn't find any blood. Both of my girls continued sobbing.

"Michele," I said, sharply, and she jerked.

"I'm fine. We're fine, I think," she said on a shuddering breath.

"Maisie, baby, it's okay," I tried soothing the still bawling toddler curled up in our laps. She had a death grip around me, her entire body shaking. The sudden scent of urine hit my nose, and I glanced down to see the wet spot on my jeans. Aw, Jesus, my poor little girl. We remained huddled on the sidewalk. Pounding footsteps grew louder.

"Shit, Pablo. Are you guys alright?" The harshly whispered question came from my right. My eyes jerked over to meet Oliver's gaze, who was squatting next to Michele.

"We're okay." I glanced down at her. Her eyes were glazed with shock. I focused back on the man on her other side. "What the fuck just happened?"

"Drive-by. Spanish Serpents based on the glimpse of the red bandana wrapped around the passenger's forehead I caught sight of before I dove for cover."

Goddamn it. "Anyone hit?" My chin tipped in the crowd's direction thirty yards away.

"Yeah, we got one dead and two flesh wounds. Cops and ambulance are on their way."

"Help me up."

I shifted my grip on Maisie and tightened my hold on her. I grasped Oliver's palm, and he heaved me to my feet, causing her to whimper and tighten her hold around my neck to nearly choking. A sharp pain raced up my thigh, and my breath caught. I grit my teeth. Once I was steady and trusted my legs to hold me *and* her, I reached down for Michele. "Come on, love."

She finally blinked and focused. Her hand settled in

mine and I gently tugged her up to standing. Her eyes met Oliver's.

"River?" She whispered.

He rubbed the back of his neck sheepishly, glancing around to make sure we weren't within earshot of anyone. "It's Oliver, actually," he said in a low voice.

"Can we please save the introductions for later? " I bit out.

"Of course, yeah, sorry. I need to go back and check on the two that were shot, but when I saw you guys, I had to make sure you hadn't been hit."

"Thanks, I appreciate it. Now, go, before people start paying too much attention to us." Hopefully the people all gathered near the front of the building were more focused on taking care of the injured than they were on why Oliver was making sure we were alright.

Michele remained rigid next to me, her gaze following my undercover agent as he jogged back to the growing crowd. She turned her eyes to me, and I flinched at the accusation and hurt shining back at me. *Fuck.* I could see the wheels spinning in her head and she wasn't liking whatever conclusion she was coming to. "You two know each other."

It wasn't a question. "It's not a good idea for us to talk about this out here. Can we please wait until we go inside? We need to take care of Maisie."

It was her turn to flinch, as though I was berating her for not thinking of her daughter, which was not my intention. What a clusterfuck this whole night was turning into. We walked together down the sidewalk, the sound of sirens quiet in the distance, but growing louder. We reached the front door at the same time the first police car, light flashing and illuminating the whole area, arrived. More sirens were coming.

Maisie finally stopped shaking, but she still hadn't released her hold on me. I hated her being quiet. She was going to have nightmares for god knew how long. We trudged up the stairs. Michele let us inside the apartment and locked the door.

"I'll take her," she said, reaching for Maisie, who began to whine again, her fingers tightening further.

"Shhh, everything's okay now." I rubbed her back and then smoothed her hair off the side of her face. "Hey, look at me, munchkin."

After a few more seconds of coaxing, she finally pulled her head back and met my eyes with her red, tear-stained ones. I gave her my best, most comforting smile. "That's my girl. Go with your mama and get all cleaned up. I promise I'll be right here if you need me."

She took in a shuddering breath, wetness clinging to her lashes. "You promise?"

"Cross my heart."

I transferred her into Michele's arms and the two of them disappeared down the hallway taking my heart with them. I remained standing there, doing everything I could to not punch a hole in the fucking wall. I jerked my phone out of my back pocket and hit the speed dial.

CHAPTER 22

MY HANDS TREMBLED CARRYING Maisie into the bathroom. Although I wasn't sure if it was her or me that was shaking more. My chest was so tight, and I could barely breathe, but I had to hold it together for my daughter. She was already traumatized enough. No need to add her mother having a massive panic attack to the mix.

I couldn't wrap my head around anything. Not the fact that we'd been caught in the middle of a fucking shoot out. Certainly not the fact that Pablo and River, or Oliver, as it were, knew each other. Nothing made sense. Nothing even mattered except taking care of Maisie.

Once in the bathroom, I stripped off her wet clothes, grabbed a washcloth and some soap and began cleaning her up. I wrapped her in a towel and carried her into the bedroom, helping her into a pair of pajamas. She hadn't spoken again, and I didn't want to break the silence by bringing up what happened and freaking her out. Instead, I cuddled her in bed with me, soothing her as best I could with gentle caresses on her cheek and brushing kisses across her forehead and eyelids.

Time didn't matter. We stayed cocooned beneath the blankets, just the two of us. Whatever it took to make her feel safe. Her body softened and her breathing evened out. I laid there with her a bit longer making sure she remained asleep. Gently, I eased out from beneath her body, pulling the covers up and tucking them under her chin. With one last kiss, I left the door cracked in case she got scared and needed me and headed back out to the living room. *Was Pablo still even here?*

He sat at the kitchen table, his hair mussed like he'd been running his fingers through it. His eyes were tired looking. In fact, his whole slouched posture and head propped on his fist exuded fatigue. He jerked upright at seeing me and quickly rose to his feet. He closed the distance between us, but I put my hand up to stop him. He ground to a halt.

"What's wrong?" he asked.

I stared at him in disbelief. *Was he insane?*

"You're kidding, right?" There was hysteria in my raised voice and I forced myself to temper it. I didn't need to disturb Maisie. "My daughter and I were shot at tonight. We're both going to have nightmares. No doubt I'm going to need to find her a therapist. Hell, maybe even one for myself so we're both not traumatized forever. Maisie's life was in danger because of Riv—Oliver and whatever the two of you have going on. Which, by the way, I'm really pissed about. How could you not tell me that you two know each other?"

"I couldn't," he rasped out. "I told you from the very

beginning that there were things related to my work I wasn't allowed to share with you. Oliver is undercover. I couldn't break his cover. Not even to you. I won't apologize for that."

The rational part of my brain understood and accepted why Pablo hadn't told me. It wasn't all that different from when Ines couldn't tell me she was undercover. It was literally life and death.

The irrational part, however, was still screaming outside as bullets flew around me, praying one of them wasn't going to hit me or my daughter. *God, why did my chest hurt so bad?* My hand flew up, and I laid it over my heart. My heartbeat was pounding like a bass drum inside my ears. The noise was so loud they throbbed. *Why couldn't I breathe?* My eyes jerked up, and I met Pablo's gaze. Black spots danced in my vision. Had I been shot and didn't know it?

"Michele," he barked out, taking a step closer. And another. Buzzing sounded inside my brain. I could feel myself moving, but it was like someone else was controlling me. I was pushed down onto a chair and gentle hands guided my head between my knees. There was a voice, but I couldn't make out what it was saying over the whooshing sounds.

Finally Pablo's voice penetrated. His touch too. He knelt next to me, hands gently palming the sides of my head, fingers brushing my hair back. "Breathe. That's it. Just keep breathing, baby. In and out. Nice and easy. Slow it down."

I concentrated on measuring how often my chest rose and fell, keeping it even, until finally it returned to normal.

My head rose and my body followed until I was sitting upright, breaking contact with Pablo. I felt wrung out. Completely exhausted.

"Jesus, you had me worried for a minute."

I met his eyes. They were filled with fear mixed with relief. Those beautiful honey-colored eyes that I think I fell in love with first. I swallowed hard and took in a shuddering breath feeling my heart crack just a bit in my chest. Tears burned behind my lids, but I blinked them back.

"I don't think I can do this."

Pablo reared back. "Can't do what?"

"This." I gestured between us. "I knew going into this that being with you, with your job, and the kind of danger you're in, would be hard. I just didn't expect we would be in danger too. That my *daughter* would be in danger."

He scooted closer again. "Hey, it's not always like this. Tonight was just a weird coincidence. Bad timing. It could have happened whether I was involved or not. Los Lobos and the Spanish Serpents have been fighting for months, and you live in their territory."

"So this is *my* fault?" I screeched.

"What? No, I didn't mean it like that. I just meant that this could have happened at any time. We were just in the wrong place at the wrong time." He sat back on his heels.

"But it didn't happen at any time. It happened tonight with you. If Oliver didn't live here, would it have happened right in front of my building? I've been living here for months and nothing like this has occurred. Oliver's been living here for less than a month and now there's a drive-by. It's entirely possible it could have been a coincidence, but I can't trust my daughter's safety on coincidence. I just can't," I said, defeated.

"So what does this mean?" Pablo's brow furrowed in confusion.

"It means, I think we need to take a step back." I pause and take a breath for courage. "I'm falling in love with you, but I don't know if being with you is the best thing for me or Maisie. I thought I could handle you being in a dangerous job, but maybe I can't. Especially when it affects my daughter."

He stared at me like he didn't know how to process what I just said. Hell, I didn't even know what I was saying. I only knew that I needed time to think about things. I couldn't do it tonight. Not after what just happened.

Pablo braced his hand on the table and slowly rose to his feet. "You know, I told Ines that a lot of women couldn't handle dating a cop. She assured me that after everything you've been through, you were strong enough to deal with it. Since getting to know you I'd started believing her. I guess we were both wrong."

I flinched at his assessment, but I didn't defend myself. His eyes stayed on me for several beats before finally he looked away. Without another word, he turned and let himself out the front door pulling it closed with a soft click. I took in a shuddering breath, and released one just as ragged. My eyes filled with tears that poured down my cheeks faster than I could wipe them away.

On unsteady legs, I headed across the living room and locked the deadbolt and secured the chain. I managed to make it to the bathroom and wash my face, which was such a pointless activity since I couldn't stop crying. I blew my nose a few times, changed into my pajamas, and crawled into bed with Maisie. All I could do though was lie there, staring up at the ceiling while tears soaked my pillow. *What had I done?*

CHAPTER 23

"I FUCKED IT UP," I said the second Ines opened her front door. "You told me not to, but I did it anyway,"

She stared at me, rolled her eyes, and blew out a dramatic sigh. "Of course you did. Come in and tell me what happened."

I swept past her and made my way to the couch, flopping down on it and dropping my head back against the cushion. The couch dipped as Ines plopped down and pivoted to face me, tucking one leg underneath her. "Okay, spill it."

"Do you remember the guy Michele was having issues with? Her neighbor?" Ines was about to go ballistic. There was no way I could avoid it. Not and tell her everything.

"Of course. I know she didn't want you talking to him, so please tell me you didn't do that. Or if you did that you didn't keep it from her."

"Worse." I winced.

Her eyes widened. "What the fuck could be worse than that?"

I took a deep breath and just let it out. "Her neighbor is Oliver."

Three.

Two.

One.

"What the fuck do you mean, it's *Oliver*? Are you telling me that the fucking sleaze bag piece of shit who has been bothering Michele all this time is your *friend*"—she sneered the word—"Oliver?"

I didn't address her question directly. "That's not the worst of it."

"Jesus Christ," she nearly yelled, throwing her hands up in the air. "How could it actually get worse?"

The whole story started spilling out of me. "Everything has been going amazing. The three of us went to the Fiesta del Sol yesterday. We had a great time. We drove back to the apartment, and walking to her building got caught in the middle of a drive-by."

Ines gasped. "Oh my god."

"We're fine," I rushed to reassure her. "None of us were hurt, but Michele and Maisie were scared shitless. Oliver saw us and rushed over after most of the chaos had died down to make sure we were okay. Of course, I had to tell her who he was. Anyway, once we made it back into the apartment and she got Maisie settled in bed, she had a massive panic attack and then we got into a huge fight."

"What did you fight about?"

"She blamed Oliver, and by proximity, me, for putting Maisie's and her life in danger. Then she broke up with me." My shoulders dropped and I sagged against the couch in self-pity.

Ines studied me. "And? What happened after that? She

understands about being undercover and how important it is to keep the secret to make sure no one gets hurt." Ines' expression was one of puzzlement. "I don't get it. Where did you fuck up? I mean, I see her being upset that you didn't tell her about Oliver and for her to have high emotions over a shooting. What am I missing?"

I avoided her gaze. "I might have unintentionally implied that it was partly her fault for living in that neighborhood and that maybe she just wasn't strong enough to deal with dating a cop."

There was only a split second of silence before the tornado erupted. Ines jumped to her feet and rapid-fire paced directly in front of me, arms gesticulating, and spewing out words as though she were yelling at someone else.

"De todas las cosas ignorantes e idioteces que pudo haber dicho. Hubiera corrido su estúpido trasero de mi casa también. ¿Qué tan pendejo puede ser?" She whirled on me. "You're a fucking idiot."

"Based on that tirade, I figured that out," I said, drily. "Let's see if I got it right. How could I be so stupid and ignorant? And you would have kicked my idiot ass out the house too. Although, I should point out that Michele didn't kick me out. I left."

Ines' eyes spat fire. "Then I stand by everything I just said. What the fuck is wrong with you? Michele and Maisie are the best thing to happen to you and you couldn't even manage to not fuck it up. I'm actually ashamed that you would say something like that to her. After everything she's been through in her life and you called her weak?"

She didn't need to make me feel worse than I already

did. As soon as the spiteful words had left my mouth I'd regretted them. Especially because they weren't true. Not anywhere near it.

"I don't really think she's weak. You know this. It was just a hurtful thing I said in the heat of the moment." God, I was such an asshole. I'd hurt her, because I'd been hurting. I was better than that. Or at least I should have been. Fuck.

"Shouldn't Michele be the one you're telling that to instead of me?" she said snidely, and I winced.

"You're right." I rose from the couch. "I'll call her today. Talk to her. Apologize to her," I emphasized when she pursed her lips and glared.

"That's probably a good idea. I sure hope for your sake she doesn't tell you to go fuck yourself. Because that's certainly what I'd tell you if you'd spoken to me that way."

"You'd no doubt make me crawl to you on my hands and knees begging and groveling for your forgiveness."

A ruthlessness flared in Ines' eyes. "You know, that's not a bad idea. Perhaps you should consider doing that."

I sent her a strained smile, because she was probably right. I better come up with a big apology. My phone rang from my back pocket, and my heart kicked up a beat hoping it was Michele. It settled into a normal rhythm at the name. *Landon*.

"Rodriguez."

"I got your message."

"And?"

"Three nights ago, Emilio Salazar left his compound in a non-descript black SUV. A few hours later there were reports of a vehicle fire, out in the Archer Heights area. No explosion. Just a fire. Wanna take a guess what kind of vehicle it was?" Landon asked.

Fuck. "A black SUV."

"Bingo. I haven't been able to get any hits from our guy inside. Still waiting on his handler. Crawford and Brickman are trying to get a positive ID on the body found in the vehicle, but until the ME does a dental exam, since that's all that was left of the guy, we can only guess."

"You think it's him, though?"

"No one has seen or heard from him since, so I think it's a fair assumption."

"Do you think he could have staged it?" I asked. "Maybe he discovered Morales was going to betray him, so that's someone else's body, and he's gone into hiding before taking his revenge on them both. Or maybe Morales double-crossed Valesquez and is still working for Salazar and they want her to think he's dead in order to draw her out."

"Jesus, any of those are possibilities as well. What about your guy? Has he heard anything?"

"The last time I talked to him, all he'd heard was that Salazar was dead and he thinks Morales killed him after meeting with a woman. He'd boasted that he eliminated someone in their way of more money and power."

"Okay. Keep me updated if you hear anything more, and I'll let you know what I get from Brickman and Crawford about the coroner's report."

"Sounds good." I ended the call and pocketed my phone. I turned to Ines. "That was Landon. Salazar is missing and presumed dead in a car fire. The DEA are waiting on dental records and the autopsy report to confirm his identity."

"Holy shit. Maybe she really is planning on taking over."

"We won't know anything solid until she surfaces or until we get confirmation Salazar is in fact dead. I need to get going. I've got to let the Captain know, and I need to reach out to Oliver as well."

"Groveling. Don't forget the groveling," she added.

"Yes, that too. I'll talk to you soon." I rose from the couch and dropped a kiss on the top of her head. "I love you."

"Love you too. Even if you are an idiot."

CHAPTER 24

TEARS POURED down my daughter's red-splattered face as she threw yet another tantrum today. It had started in the middle of the night. She'd woken up screaming, no doubt from a nightmare, and she wanted Pablo. Nothing I did soothed her. Her screams quieted to sobs which quieted to tears, but she didn't stop until she'd cried herself back to sleep. Since then, it had been tantrum after tantrum. I'd had to call in sick to work, because she wouldn't stop kicking and screaming for me to even get her out the door to the sitter's house.

"Maisie, baby, you need to drink this." I tried giving her some Pedialyte. She'd cried so much I worried she was going to get dehydrated.

She pushed my hand holding the bottle away. "I want"—hiccuped sob—"Pablo."

I was at my wit's end and ready to join her in a crying fit as well, because I wanted him too. Instead, I laid down next to her with a blanket, rubbing her back and doing the best I could to get through this. "He's not here right now, baby. Please stop crying. It's going to be okay."

Maisie only continued crying. Finally she fell asleep again. I continued lying there not even having the energy to get up. I'd barely slept myself before she'd woken up yelling. All I'd done was replay the entire night over and over wondering what the hell went wrong.

Pablo had been right. The two gangs had been fighting with each other long before Oliver ever moved in. More than likely they'd go on fighting long after he moved out as well. Him being here or not wouldn't change that. Which meant that what happened last night could have happened any night. It could have happened just as easily on a night I'd come home late after working a double.

If anyone was at fault, it was me. I was the one who put my daughter in danger. It wasn't Oliver. It certainly wasn't Pablo.

Beside me, Maisie whimpered in her sleep. I rubbed my scratchy eyes, pushing back my own tears. They wouldn't do me any good.

The knock at the door startled me. Maisie stirred, but thankfully stayed sleeping. I slowly climbed to my feet and squinted to look through the peephole. My breath caught. I unlatched the chain, flipped the deadbolt, and then nothing separated me from Pablo, who stood in the hallway holding two boxes of chocolates, a large heart-shaped one and a twin mini-sized one. He held them both up. "I come bearing bribes."

I stepped back, pulling the door wider and he came inside, his familiar scent wafting around me. I closed the door and leaned against it.

Pablo's eyes landed on Maisie lying in the middle of

the living room floor. He turned back to me with concern. "Is everything okay?"

Hysterical laughter bubbled up through my chest. "Not really."

Pablo set the boxes of candy down and moved to stand in front of me. He started to reach for me, but he hesitated, as though not sure of his welcome. It only took that tiny movement, and I threw myself in his arms with a sob. His arms wrapped tightly around me, and I bawled against his muscled chest, soaking his gray t-shirt with my tears. He smoothed my hair and palmed the back of my head, whispering words of comfort against my temple.

"I'm sorry I said that you were to blame by living here. I'm even more sorry that I said you weren't strong enough to handle things. If anything, I'm the one who can't. I told you I wasn't any good at this relationship thing. I'm sorry for making you feel less than the absolutely amazing woman you are. I was hurt and lashing out. It wasn't fair to you. I'm sorry."

"No." I shook my head, smearing wetness everywhere. "I'm the one who's sorry. I blamed you and Oliver for something completely out of your control. That shooting could have happened anytime. It's nobody's fault except those stupid gangs. I was scared, and I wasn't thinking straight. I didn't mean to blame you. I know you couldn't tell me about Oliver being undercover. I get it."

Pablo dipped down and palmed my head, tipping it gently so I was looking up at him. His thumbs brushed the lingering tears from my cheeks. "Did you mean the other thing you said though?"

"What's that?"

"About falling in love with me?"

185

My lashes fluttered and my eyes shifted to glance away before I slowly raised them again to meet his gaze. Heat flushed across my chest and cheeks. I swallowed. "Yes. I meant it."

"Good," he said, his expression serious. "Because I'm falling in love with you too. Hell, I'm pretty sure I already fell."

A watery smile crossed my face. Pablo bent his head and brought his mouth to mine. This kiss was different than all the others we'd shared. It was full of apologies, promises, and love. It was his hopes and my dreams all mixed together in a giant rainbow of colors. It was my heart touching his and becoming one. My fingers danced along his muscled back, while his strong hands still cradled my head, holding me tightly to him as though he never wanted to let me go.

A cry from behind Pablo broke us apart. I rushed over to Maisie who began howling again. I lifted her in my arms.

"Shit, is she okay?"

Her eyes landed on him, and she started wrestling and fighting and reaching for him, yelling his name. His panicked eyes met mine while I tried desperately to keep her from falling. I transferred her over to him, and she clung to him like a second skin, sobbing huge tears against his shoulder. Her legs were wrapped around his waist, ankles locked. The same with her arms around his neck. She sobbed for what felt like hours, but was, in reality, only a few minutes, until finally they subsided into quiet hiccups.

Pablo paced back and forth between the kitchen and the living room, the two of them still holding each other tight. I'd long ago collapsed into an exhausted heap on the couch. My feelings stung that he'd been able to comfort Maisie when I hadn't been able to, but then I felt guilty because it was obvious he was who she'd needed. I was going to have to learn to share. I'd never been in love before. Not like this. It scared the shit out of me.

Weight settled next to me, and I looked over. Pablo had taken a seat at the other end and Maisie sat sideways in his lap, her head resting on his chest and her middle two fingers in her mouth. She hadn't sucked her fingers in months.

"Don't worry, mama, everything's all better now, isn't that right, munchkin?" he kissed the top of her nodding head. "We had a nice talk and Maisie knows it's okay to be scared, but that no one is going to hurt her. Even if I'm not always here."

I smiled gently at the two of them. "I'm glad you're feeling better, baby. I love you."

"Love you, Mama." Her words were garbled around her fingers.

"I love you both," Pablo added, reaching out with a free hand and laying it on top of mine.

My eyes leaped up to meet his. I blinked back tears. "I love you too."

I scooted right up to his side, and he wrapped an arm around my shoulders tucking me in tight. I held onto Maisie's hand and the three of us sat there, connected together, like our own little family.

CHAPTER 25

I SAT at my desk looking at old cases, when Oliver came running in out of breath. "Holy shit, have you talked to the Captain?"

"Not lately. What's going on?"

"An anonymous tip came in providing evidence that Ricardo Morales not only murdered Emilio Salazar, but said that if we wanted to arrest him, he would be at a house over on south Spaulding Avenue this afternoon. It's allegedly one of the places where he stores his drug supply. Cap wants all of us saddled up and ready to go."

"Are you for real? How do we know this isn't a setup or some wild goose chase?"

"I don't know what the evidence was or the exact nature of the tip, but whatever it was, it's enough to convince the judge to give us a warrant to move on this thing."

Christ. I hadn't been out in the field on a bust since I'd been shot. My palms began to sweat and my stomach churned.

"Hey, don't look like that," Oliver said. "It's going to be fine. I got your back."

I shook off the uneasy feeling and nodded. I could do this.

We headed into the weapons and equipment room and donned our Kevlar vests and additional ammunition as well as a second sidearm. Several of our colleagues joined us, including Peterman, who sent me a sideways glance. I tried not to let it annoy me. Instead, I took a few deep breaths and went back to my ritual.

I did a mental checklist of all my equipment: vest, weapons, ammunition, communication device. I kept my breathing even as I sat on the bench with my elbows on my knees and my head bent. Once I felt ready, I rose to my feet and approached Peterman.

"I know you've been...concerned about my return to duty, but I want you to know you don't have anything to worry about. I don't plan on taking any unnecessary risks. Not for myself or anyone on the team. I have no desire to play hero. I want everyone to come out this safe. I didn't want you to have any worries on that account." I reached out to shake his hand.

He jerked back a bit in surprise. He put his hand in mine. "I appreciate that, Rodriguez. It's good to know we all have each other's back."

I nodded and turned to close my locker, ignoring Oliver's stare. The Captain entered the room and gave us a rundown on how the raid would play out.

"We're heading to a house on south Spaulding Avenue. Defense formation spread out on each side. You four"—he pointed at me and the three guys at my side—"I want you guys in the front. You other four take the back. We'll enter from both sides of the house. Sweep the first and second floors and do what you can to peaceably take down any suspects. There is rumored to be approximately four million dollars' worth of illegal narcotics and tens of millions of dollars in cash stored there. We have reason to believe that not only will Ricardo Morales be inside, but also all of his top enforcers. Be safe in there."

Once we arrived, we all hustled into position. For a moment, deja vu hit. Oliver at my front and Sharp at my back. That rush of adrenaline. The thrill of the chase. It all came pouring in.

On its heels though were visions of Michele and Maisie, and it settled my emotions to a much more even-keel. It was no longer just me. I had people who needed me to come home more than I needed that surge of power. I breathed in calm just as the signal came.

The team leader banged on the door. "Chicago PD. Open up."

Like a well-oiled machine, we kicked in the door and burst through, scattering like someone dumped marbles on the floor. The second team raced upstairs. Oliver and I swept the rooms on the right while Peterman and Sharp swept the ones on the left.

Rapid gunfire came from a backroom. "Down! Get down on the ground," someone screamed. Cautiously, we finished panning the rooms, until we met the other two in the large, completely gutted, kitchen. All the cupboards and cabinets had been removed, as well as appliances, and instead replaced with open shelves stacked with wrapped bundles of pills. A large table covered in stacks of bills and guns stood off to one side of the room.

On the floor, in the middle of everything was Ricardo

Morales and two of his men. Seeing them cuffed and secured on the floor, I nudged Oliver.

"Let's do another sweep."

We carefully made our way upstairs and were greeted by the rest of our team.

"No one's up here," Banks said.

"Are you sure?" Oliver asked.

"Yeah. We swept every room. They were all clear. Why?"

"Because if the intel we got from the anonymous source is fully accurate and Morales was here with his top enforcers, then we're one man short," he said.

"Shit. We're missing something then." I turned and headed back downstairs, the men following behind me. We went room to room again, but there was no one hiding in any closets or under any beds. We passed a door in the hallway, and I paused, directing attention with the muzzle of my gun.

"Does this house have a basement?" I lowered my voice.

"Son of a bitch," Oliver hissed. "I don't know."

We plastered against the wall, and slowly I reached to turn the door handle. The hinges creaked as I pushed it open. Darkness greeted us. Staying behind the cover of the wall, I reached around in search of a light switch, found it, and flipped it up. I shared a look with Oliver.

"Chicago PD. If anyone is down there, you have nowhere to go. Come out now with your hands up." I repeated my words in Spanish just in case. Shuffling sounds came from below. I inhaled and nodded before quickly poking my head around the door frame to get a look downstairs. My head jerked back at the sight of the gun, and then a bullet whizzed by. In unison, Oliver and I pivoted and opened fire down the basement stairs. A bark of pain followed, and we took the opportunity to make our move.

Weapons pointed, we stormed the basement, the naked suspect on the ground and bleeding, his gun lying next to him. I approached, kicked the pistol away from him, and flipped him on his stomach, handcuffing his hands to his back.

"Sweet mother of God."

I glanced over to see horror written on Oliver's face as he stared from the doorway into some type of walled-off room. My eyes took in the entire basement. There were at least five more doors which looked to lead into additional walled off rooms. What the hell was down here? Sharp appeared at the top of the stairs, took in the scene, and made his way down.

"You okay, Rodriguez?" he asked.

"Yeah," I said, distracted, my eyes still on Oliver. I glanced down at the cuffed man. "Watch him, will you?"

Leaving him to keep an eye on our suspect, I moved over to stand next to Oliver and looked at what still had his rapt, horrified attention. I sucked in a breath. *Jesus.* An obviously dead woman, possibly in her late teens or early twenties, was propped naked against a wall, a collar around her neck attached to the wall by a chain. A needle lay on the floor next to her, and rubber tubing was strapped tightly around her arm inches above her track-mark dotted elbow.

A moan from the adjoining room caught our attention. Weapons at the ready, we made our way down the narrowed pathway, pausing in front of the neighboring door. *Fuck.* We moved to the next one and the next.

"Sharp," I yelled over my shoulder. "We need more medics. Now. Get some of the guys down here. Bring blankets, and see if you can find some water."

Oliver hadn't said another word until he reached the last open door. A whimpering cry came from inside. Pounding footsteps rushed down the stairs, but I ignored them. The men would see what we'd already found soon enough. Instead, I focused on Oliver who stepped inside the room. I quickly checked the remaining two rooms and found the same of what I'd seen in the previous two.

I stopped in the doorway my friend had entered. He was removing the collar from the naked woman sitting in the bed. The second he had it off, she threw herself into arms, barely able to breathe through her bawling. I didn't see any track marks on her, but based on the cuts and bruises on her body she had not been gently treated. Fresh blood dotted the bed, and I averted my gaze. I glanced at the suspect lying out in the middle of the floor, Sharp still standing over him, and I wanted to murder him.

Sirens grew louder until they were right outside the house. Footsteps above me, and then the paramedics were rushing down the stairs.

"We have one dead woman and several others who seem to be under the influence of narcotics, most likely heroin. Chained and potential victims of sexual assault. Officer Garrison is in the last room on the right with one of the women. Also suspected victim of recent assault."

Being down here was getting to me. I avoided looking inside the rooms as I headed over to the open space.

"I'll take him," I said of the suspect. I reached down

and hauled him to his feet before dragging him upstairs. He got tossed into the back of a patrol car none too gently before I returned to the house. A couple members of the forensics team had arrived and were processing and bagging the evidence. All I wanted to do was go home and squeeze my girls tight.

Peterman appeared at my side.

"Hey," he said. "Good job today."

"Thanks," I replied.

I moved around the scene until everything was tagged and loaded up for the evidence room. Oliver finally made his way upstairs, the girl still attached to him, but now covered in a blanket. He helped her outside and into the back of an ambulance. He tried leaving her with the female paramedic, but she wouldn't let him go. He sent me a pleading look for some help.

"Go," I told him. "I'll let the Captain know what's going on and where you are."

He nodded and the door closed, shutting them inside before the ambulance took off. Our two teams jumped back into the back of the department vans and headed to the precinct. I hurried to unload all my stuff. Then I was gone and on my way to Michele's, hoping she didn't mind me dropping by unannounced. Because after tonight, I needed to see her.

CHAPTER 26

I HADN'T EXPECTED the knock. Dropping my book on the couch, I made my way over to the door and peeked out the peephole. I quickly unlocked it and let Pablo in. Before I could blink he pulled me into his chest, breathing deeply against my hair. I wrapped my arms around him, and we just stood there. The expression that had been on his face had me worried. It was obvious something was wrong. There had been pure misery written across it. I hugged him that much tighter and he responded in kind.

After several minutes, he loosened his hold. "You have no idea how much I needed that."

I brushed his hair back off his face and raised up on tiptoe to press my lips to his. "Then I'm glad I could give it to you. Come on, let's go have a seat, and if you want to talk about anything you can. You don't have to though. We can just sit. Whatever you need."

He moved into the living room, tugging off his gun belt and laying it to the side while I closed and locked the door and then joined him on the couch, pushing my books out of the way. I tucked myself against his side, just being here if he needed me, but not pushing. It was at least five minutes before he finally spoke.

"We went on a bust tonight. My first since being shot. I was scared shitless going in, but thoughts of you and Maisie calmed me. Things went smooth. We took down the suspects with relative ease. None of us were hurt. For a short time, I felt good. Back to my old self." Pablo paused, but I kept my silence. "Then we discovered something that made me want to vomit. Drugged-up women chained to walls in the basement like animals. They were all stoned out of their minds. Well, except the one who had overdosed."

I shuddered at the image and my eyes burned with unshed tears for women I didn't know. God, how awful for them. It was something I would never wish on another human being. It didn't surprise me that Pablo had been horrified. I was too, and I could only imagine.

"How do you do it?" I asked. "Seeing that kind of thing, I mean? How do you do it day in and day out? I couldn't handle it."

"We don't typically see that kind of thing in narcotics. I mean, we might run across someone in a drug house that has overdosed, and certainly ones high as a kite, but as horrible as it sounds you almost become numb to it. What I saw tonight wasn't anything I'd ever encountered before. I never want to again." Pablo's gaze was unfocused, his voice soft.

I cuddled closer, wrapping myself around him trying to comfort him in any way I could. Words could only do so much. Pablo didn't say anything further, so I held him tight to at least let him know I was here if he wanted to keep talking. We sat in the quiet, the only sound the ticking of the clock on the stove and our breathing. Soon, a soft snore came from Pablo. I glanced up and his eyes were closed, his expression much more relaxed than when he'd arrived. I must have dozed as well, because my body jerked, and my eyes flew open. Nothing had changed, except Pablo was awake again as well.

"I'm sorry I fell asleep on you," he said. "I know you're trying to study for your test tomorrow."

"Don't worry about it. You needed the rest, and I needed the break. I've been studying all night."

He shifted a bit and pulled me onto his lap. His hand rested on my hip and my arms went around his shoulders, my fingers playing with the hair curled around his collar.

"Thank you for listening," he said.

"Of course. I may not know what to say, but I will always listen." I leaned forward and pressed my lips to his.

This kiss began as a way for me to offer a small amount of comfort. It was obvious he'd been deeply affected by what happened tonight. I wanted to take his thoughts away from what he'd seen, even if it was only for a brief time. I flicked my tongue out, tracing the seam, teasing him, encouraging him to let me in. He opened for me, but I kept this kiss gentle. I lightly caressed the inside of his mouth, pulling back when he moved to deepen the connection.

I pressed tiny kisses along the corner of his lips, dotted his cheeks, his nose, both his eyelids before tracking the same path I'd just taken. Pablo's fingers speared my hair, while the grip of his hand on my hip tightened, and he tried to control our movements.

"Let me," I whispered against his mouth.

His touch eased, and I shifted so that I straddled him. It seemed like this was going to be a common theme when we were here. Never before had I wanted my own bed in my own room more than I did now. I continued ghosting sweet kisses over his face, before taking his lips again. My hands cradled his cheeks. Our hips rocked together, but I could already tell I wasn't going to be satisfied with a repeat of the last time we'd been in this position. What had started out as comfort had quickly morphed into something more. Something needier.

"Condom?" I asked against his mouth.

He pulled his head and stared questioningly at me. "I didn't come over here for this. You know that, right?"

With a finger, I brushed the stray curl off his forehead and traced his skin. "Of course I know that. I love you, and you love me. You're also hurting, and I want to ease that hurt. I also need you. I don't want you to think about anything else for a little while except how much I love you."

Pablo's eyes flickered over my face. "Are you sure?"

I answered him with a kiss. We sipped at each other's lips, tasting, savoring. He laid me back on the couch and then reached for his wallet, pulling out a condom and setting it on the end table behind my head. I raised my hips so he could tug down my pajama shorts and underwear. He made to lower his head to my center, but I stopped him with a light touch.

"As much as I want you to take your time and do all the dirty things I've been dreaming about for the months since I met you, this first time should probably be just the main attraction," I told him with a cheeky grin. My eyes darted in the direction of the hallway and my room. "I would hate to be interrupted during the sneak peek of what's coming next and miss out on a performance I've really been looking forward to."

Pablo buried his face against my thigh trying to stifle the laughter spilling from him. He got himself under control quickly and nodded. "You're probably right. If need be, we can take a break during intermission and maybe squeeze in the second act."

"Tonight might just be your lucky night."

His expression turned serious. "No might about it. Every night I get to spend with you is lucky."

My heart swelled, and I leaned up for one more kiss. "I love you."

"I love you, too."

Pablo raised up and grabbed the condom, while I worked on his belt buckle and loosened his pants. He tugged them down enough to free his cock. My eyes worshipped the sight of it and a surge of disappointment hit that I wouldn't be able to spend time touching and exploring him. He tore the wrapper open and slid the latex down his length. I grabbed the throw from the back of the couch and tossed it over our bodies. No need to risk horribly embarrassing questions from Maisie if, god forbid, she interrupted us.

Pablo settled between my legs, his shaft hitting me in the right spot. He leaned down and laid his lips on mine. We kissed while our hands roamed over each other. His disappeared beneath the blanket, and my breath caught. A finger flicked over my clit, and pleasure ricocheted through my body. I separated my legs as best I could in this position, pushing myself upward in hopes of getting more of his touch. Pablo didn't disappoint. He circled and rubbed the tiny bundle of flesh, and with each gasp and moan repeated the motion that caused it, learning what pressure and direction pleased me the most.

Wetness poured from me as he lashed his tongue against mine while his fingers continued their sensual assault below. My fingers threaded through his locks, and I clung to him, deepening the kiss. A moan of pleasure rumbled out of my chest and Pablo swallowed it down, softening the sound. His lips trailed from my mouth to the crease in my neck, and I bit my lip to keep from crying out at the sensation. With a free hand, I reached between us and circled his throbbing cock.

"I need you inside. Please," I begged, trying to guide him to where I wanted him most.

At last, he lined himself up with my entrance and slowly pushed forward inch by agonizing inch until he was fully seated deep inside. I sucked in shallow breaths, and wrapped my free leg around him, just under his butt and then I pushed up, pulling him down at the same time. The air seized in my lungs, and Pablo let out a gruff groan.

"Fuck, you're tight. You feel so good," he rasped against my neck.

I nipped his ear. "Move, damn it. Fuck me. Please."

Those few words were all it took to ignite the fire. Pablo began a steady thrusting, hitting me in that one spot with each one. Sweat-slicked hair stuck to my forehead and his as our passion rose. I buried my face in his neck, holding back my cries of ecstasy as I was swept higher in the maelstrom of pleasure. With only a few flicks to my clit, my body tensed and then shook with my release. Colors exploded behind my eyelids and I whimpered as pleasure racked my entire body. Pablo thrust a few more times and slammed his mouth down on my shoulder. He went rigid, and a groan vibrated from his throat against my shirt, muffling the sound.

His weight sagged against me, and he made to take some of it off me, but I tightened my hold on him. "Not yet, please. Stay."

I loved the feel of him on top of me. The heaviness. I wanted to hold on to this feeling a little while longer. I breathed in the scent of Pablo and sex that lingered in the air. My pussy still pulsed with need. He shifted and let out a gruff sound.

"If you keep squeezing me like that I can't be responsible for my actions."

I clenched down, tightening myself around him. "Like that?"

"God woman, you're killing me."

That made me giggle. I finally took pity on him and loosened my hold. He pulled out of me and while he disposed of the condom, I quickly grabbed my clothes off the floor and tugged them back on. Pablo returned from the bathroom, thankfully without issue, and sat next to me on the couch. I tugged him down until his head rested on my lap. I fingered his hair, plucking at the loose curls I loved so much.

"Are you feeling any better?" I asked, staring down at him.

"I am, thanks to you."

"Good."

"Mama?" A sleepy Maisie appeared around the side of the couch rubbing her tired eyes. Pablo sat up and he and I exchanged relieved looks that she hadn't come out five minutes earlier.

"Hey, baby. Why aren't you in bed?"

"I heard a noise, and I got scareded." She crawled up in between us and curled her small body against mine, her head under my shoulder and her feet tucked under Pablo's thigh. Within seconds she was right back to sleep.

"Good lord, I wish I had the sleep of babes," Pablo joked.

"You and me both. She's always been like that. Wakes up in the middle of the night, and falls back to sleep in seconds."

"It was probably me in the bathroom that woke her up. I'm sorry. I thought I'd been quiet."

I snorted. "More than anything it was probably all the grunting and groaning you were doing out here that woke her up."

Pablo's head whipped in my direction. I tried desperately to hold in the bubble of laughter, but the look of affront on his face was too much. It escaped, and I covered my mouth trying to quiet it. My whole body shook with the effort.

He mock-growled. "Your daughter won't always be between us to protect you. Just wait. Next time we'll see who does all the grunting and groaning. I'm going to keep you on the edge of pleasure you'll be cursing and screaming at me to let you come."

"Do you promise?" I nearly bounced with anticipation.

Pablo's mouth dropped in shock, but he quickly recovered. "I love you, you know that?"

I leaned over my daughter for a kiss. "I love you too. "

CHAPTER 27

"STILL NO WORD ON VALESQUEZ?" I asked Landon.

"Nothing. It's crazy. I finally heard from our under-cover agent's handler, and even the agent doesn't know what's going on. The cartel is in utter chaos right now and has been since Salazar's death. His second-in-command, Martínez, has gone into hiding, and no one knows why or where. They're currently without a leader. The compound where he lived has been abandoned. Staff is gone as is security. I'm assuming they're regrouping. Got some intel out of Mexico that a couple men from down there are crossing the border and may be arriving in Chicago in the next few days. Don't know yet if they're on Salazar's or Valesquez's payroll."

That woman had truly done some major destruction. "I guess there's nothing any of us can do but wait until the dust settles and see who's left standing."

"We're blind right now," Landon said. "The Spanish Serpents apparently are back in the game now that Los Lobos is lacking a leader as well."

Earlier today, I'd discovered the evidence we'd received that got us the warrant for the Morales raid. A hat- and sunglasses-wearing dark-haired woman had strolled straight into our local precinct and handed an unmarked package to the officer at the front desk. He opened it and began flipping through the enclosed photos. When he looked up, the woman had disappeared. Surveillance footage caught her entering and exiting the building, but she'd kept her face averted away from the cameras, and no one had been able to pick her up on any of the street cams surrounding us.

"Yeah, they're still trying to find the woman who dropped off all the photos and that video," I stated.

All the pictures had been of Ricardo Morales inside the same house we'd raided, surrounded by drugs, money, and guns. On the back of each one were the initials M.L.V. There had also been a DVD showing him dousing the inside of a black SUV with some type of accelerant and striking the match. Reports showed the gas tank had been emptied, which was why there hadn't been an explosion.

"You know, it makes me wonder if she didn't discover those women locked in the basement and decided that she could get rid of two of her problems in one swoop. Based on her history, my guess is she wasn't too keen on keeping a working relationship with Morales. As someone sold at the age of fourteen, she probably wanted to see him suffer. Instead, she was smart about it. She let him kill the half-brother who'd sold her *and* got him arrested not only for Salazar's murder, but also for a shit ton of drug and weapons charges. It's pretty brilliant if you ask me," Landon said.

She fit right in with our family. All the women knew

they were just as capable and smart, often smarter, as the men in their life. It seemed all of the Rodriguez or Thomas men had our work cut out for us. None of us would change our women for anything though.

"It's entirely possible. I still want to know what her end game is."

Landon sighed. "You and me both. It would certainly solve a lot of our problems. Alright, I need to get going. Keep in touch."

"Will do."

I hung up the desk phone and picked up my keys, ready to head home. Michele and Maisie were coming over for dinner and there was something important I wanted to talk to her about. I was nervous as fuck though.

"Hey, you on your way out?"

I glanced up to see Oliver heading toward me. It had been a few days since I'd last spoke to him. The day after the raid, he'd been called up to the front desk and then had taken the next couple days off. He looked tired.

"I'm meeting Michele and Maisie at the house in about an hour. Hey, congratulations on getting all that evidence against Los Lobos. We got in, what twelve arrests? I think with all the drugs and money recovered this is one of the biggest drug busts we've had since we took down Ortega three years ago."

He took a seat in the chair on the opposite side of my desk. "Thanks. Morales got sloppy. He started bragging about too many things around too many people. I suspect he thought he'd be under the cartel's protection or something. That with this new deal with Salazar and then Valesquez he and his gang were untouchable."

"Add in those women we found, and Morales is going

to be put away for a very long time. Speaking of, how's the one you went to the hospital with? Was she okay?" I asked.

Oliver flinched, not meeting my eye, and rubbed the back of his neck. "Traumatized, of course. She'd been chained in that room for a week, which she said was lucky for her. From the sounds of it, she was the last one that had been taken. The other women had been in there far longer than she had, but she didn't know exactly. They weren't allowed to talk to one another."

"Christ. Those poor women."

We both sat in silence, reliving that day and seeing the condition we'd found them in. I don't know how she could have counted herself lucky. Then again, she was still alive, so maybe that counted for something. Oliver rose. "I won't keep you. I know you're anxious to get to your lady and your kid. Have a good one."

"Huh, oh, yeah, you too," I said distracted, my brain hung up on hearing him call Maisie my kid. God, that was one of the best sounding things in the world. A slow smile began to spread across my face. If I had anything to say about it, she would be mine.

For the second time I picked up my keys and headed out to my car, both anxious and nervous about tonight. Whatever happened was going to change the rest of my life.

CHAPTER 28

THERE WERE an awful lot of cars in front of Pablo's house. Ines and Brody were supposed to be having dinner with us as well, but from the looks of it, the entire Rodriguez and Thomas clans were here. Not that I minded. I loved all of Pablo's family. It was just a little intimidating being around all of them. Considering how things were going with us though, I better get used to it. *Was this a special occasion?*

I helped Maisie out of her car seat, and we headed to the front door. I rang the bell and waited, while my daughter danced excitedly next to me. It opened wide and conversation and laughter spilled out.

"How are my two favorite girls?" Pablo sang out, bending down to pick up Maisie. Once she was in his arms, he leaned over and gave me a kiss.

"I hope we didn't keep everyone waiting. I didn't realize the whole family was going to be here," I said after he closed the door behind us.

"Neither did I. They were all here when I showed up."

The three of us headed to the family den where everyone was gathered. They all waved at our entrance. Pablo set Maisie down and she rushed over and started playing with Cristina and Nicholás.

"Hey, you made it," Ines came over and pulled me into a hug. "Brody and I kind of hijacked your and Pablo's dinner plans, I'm sorry."

"I don't mind."

"Food's just about ready. We were going to head to the kitchen as soon as you got here. The kids are getting hangry," she said.

"Good god, we don't want that to happen." Pablo shuddered and Ines smacked his arm.

"Marguerite will let you deal with her two if you don't watch what you say."

He scoffed. "I'm the favorite uncle. They wouldn't act like assholes around me."

"Hey, I heard that," Victor butted in, Estelle at his side.

She leaned over and stage-whispered, "Are you sure you're ready to deal with this family? You still have time to run. I'll hold them back while you get a head start."

Pablo playfully nudged her out of the way with his elbow and wrapped his arm around my waist, tugging me against his side. "Don't you dare give her any ideas. I finally caught her, and now that I have, I have no intention of losing her."

He emphasized his words with a kiss to my temple.

"I guess you're stuck now," Victor joked.

"Don't you worry. I'm right where I want to be," I replied.

"Ha," Pablo spit out. "See, I told you she wasn't going anywhere."

"Lucky us," Ines added.

"Alright, everyone, dinner is ready," Ernesto called from the doorway wearing a bright white apron tied around his waist. Pablo's niece and nephew jumped up and tore out of the den screaming and hollering while their mother followed after them with a shake of her head.

Ernesto's eyes lit up when they landed on me, and he hurried over. "Hola, my lovely, I'm so happy to see you." He squeezed my shoulder and brushed a kiss across both my cheeks before pulling back and glancing around. "Where is the pequeño mono?"

I pointed to where Maisie was half-hidden behind Manuel and Brody, squatting and moving a few dolls around that were sitting in tiny chairs around a tiny table apparently having a tea party. She must have been satisfied with their placement, because she stood and looked around. There were a few less people in here than when we'd arrived. Her brow scrunched and then she was running over to us. She hooted in excitement. "Hola Mister 'nesto," she yelled right before colliding with his legs and wrapping her arms around them in a hug.

He patted her lovingly on the head. "Very good pequeño mono. Where did you learn that?"

"Mama told me. I wanted to s'prise you with my Spanish. That's all I know, so you have to teached me some more."

"I will be happy to," he said. "Are you hungry? I made a special meal for all of us."

"My belly is always hungry."

"Well then, why don't we go join the others?"

While we'd been talking to Ernesto, everyone had left the den and headed into the kitchen. Like we had at the birthday party, we formed a long line, slowly moving through until we all had our food and then were seated at the table. Much more relaxed this time around, I participated in all the conversations around me, laughing and having a great time. Soon dinner began to wind down. A tinkling sound grew louder, and our attention turned to Ines who was clinking her knife against her glass.

"I'm so glad everyone was able to get together tonight. I know there's a lot of us." She gently bounced Zoey who was seated in her lap. Her eyes danced to mine and they twinkled with delight. "I asked papá to bring you all here, because...Brody and I are getting married."

She squealed and stuck her hand out in front of her, wiggling her fingers and showing off the ring that now graced her third finger. All the women, including me, gasped, all of us vying to get a good look at it, while the men offered their congratulations. She handed Zoey over to Brody and jumped from her chair to come around the table and show it off to everyone. It was absolutely stunning. A single cushion diamond set in a v-shaped band inlaid with tiny diamonds.

Once we'd all gotten a good look, Pablo and I helped clear the table and clean up the kitchen. Maisie had run off with the other kids.

"Hey, you," Pablo snuck up behind me, wrapping his arms around my belly and nuzzling the crease in my neck. "Why don't we go outside? It's a little more private out there."

He led me outside, and we sat at the same table where everything had started. Unlike that first day, the silence between us was comfortable. Easy. Just being near him was enough.

"I wanted to ask you something, and I want you to think about it."

My eyes widened with a bit of panic. "Okay," I answered nervously.

"You and Maisie are the best things to ever happen to me. Until I met you, I never thought I'd find a woman who was more perfect for me. You are so easy to love. So is your daughter. I want to spend all my time with you and her." He paused and took a deep breath. "You work harder than anyone I know to provide for your daughter. But I want to help take some of the burden off of you."

Pablo reached over and tugged me out of my chair and into his lap. "I want to take care of you both. I worry about you living in that neighborhood. We both know it's not the safest."

I started to speak, but he pressed a finger to my lips. "I don't mean that as some snide remark about any choices you've made. You know how much I admire you, and if you don't, then I need to do a better job of showing you."

"You do show me. All the time. You show me how much you care and love me. And my daughter."

"Good, because I do love you. My father knew he loved my mother the moment he saw her. There was definitely something there, a spark, from that first time we met, and it's only grown bigger, brighter, and hotter ever since. I want to be your husband one day. I want to be Maisie's papá, and I want to be papá to any more kids we might have."

My throat clogged with emotions. I wanted all that too, but I was scared.

"I know that's a lot to throw at you all at once. More

than I'd actually planned on saying yet, because I can tell just by your expression that you're freaking out a bit."

Choked laughter escaped, because he was right.

"So let's start small, and then we can build and go from there. Again, think about your answer before you give it. I want you and Maisie to move in. Here, in this house, with us. I've already talked to my father about it, and he is beyond excited. A ridiculous amount of excited if you want to know the truth. He says he's missed having all of us here, and I know how unhappy he would be living alone. He adores you and Maisie and he would love nothing more than to become an abuelo again."

This was all so overwhelming. Even if I wanted to, I couldn't answer right away. I'd never expected this. "But Maisie's school? And her sitter? They're all near our apartment and my work."

"Taken care of. Our entire family does everything for each other. No questions asked. We want you to be a part of this family. Marguerite and Ines have offered to watch Maisie any time, whether you're at work or if we go out on a date night. She'll have any number of aunts and uncles who can take her to pre-school and pick her up, plus me. I don't work far from there. Once she finishes, we can look at transferring her to a preschool nearer to here."

"Wow," I breathed out. "You've really thought this through, haven't you?"

"I have. It's all I've been thinking about. I want to start my life with you, and I hope you want to start it with me as well. So, think about it. Do whatever you consider to be the best for you and Maisie, and no matter what your answer is, I will support it and you no matter what."

The sliding glass door opened, and Ines popped her head out. "Did you ask her yet?"

"Are you kidding me right now?" Pablo yelled over his shoulder, and I started laughing. "Go away, for Christ's sake."

She huffed but did as he said.

"Yes," I said.

Pablo's head snapped in my direction. "What?"

"I said yes."

He sat there in stunned silence and then he jumped to his feet, bringing me with him and spun us around in a circle. "Yes! She said yes," he hollered.

I threw my head back in glee. Pablo stopped spinning and set me on my feet, cradling my face, and plastering his lips against mine. "I love you so much. You won't regret this, I promise."

Knowing Pablo, I believed him. I was scared to death, because we seemed to be moving so fast, but everything felt right. I loved him. Maisie loved him. We were becoming part of the kind of family I'd always wished I'd had.

"I love you. You make me incredibly happy."

"If you're okay with it, let's go tell that little girl in there."

Pablo took my hand, and nothing had ever felt more right. My daughter and I were finally where we belonged.

EPILOGUE

One week ago

I WASN'T ready to leave. Not really. Leaving meant going back out there. It meant dealing with shit I didn't think I could deal with yet. Already, my stomach hurt, and there was a stabbing pain in the vicinity of my heart that made me think I was having a heart attack, even though I knew I wasn't. It was a pain I'd become intimately familiar with over the last two years. Since I'd been off my meds, it had become an all too frequent occurrence. The only cure was to breathe through it like the countless therapists I'd been to had coached me to do.

A bitter, nearly hysterical laugh bubbled out of me. If Dr. Leahy could see me sitting here in this bed, he'd probably just write me a few more prescriptions for Xanax and call it a day. He'd been my last in a cycle of terrible doctors who'd done nothing but give me more pills. Therapist. Doctors. It's all my life had been. No one knew what the fuck to do with me.

Here I was, about to be discharged from the hospital, and I was even more fucked up than before I got here. Although I'm not sure that was saying much. There came a scratch at the door, and then it opened, that annoyingly perky fucking nurse popping her head in.

"Oh good, you're awake," she said, entering my room, with a thousand-watt smile I wanted to punch off her face.

Anger issues were just one of my many problems. I returned her expression with a no doubt patronizing smirk.

"I have all your discharge paperwork here," she continued, white teeth still brightly displayed. "The doctor wanted me to go over it with you one more time before he signed in. Once that's done, you're free to leave."

Yay, me. I barely listened while she rattled off all the doctor's instructions. Prescription—check. Wound care—check. Referral to yet another therapist—check. I nodded in all the appropriate places, my mind already wandering. I didn't really care about a word she was saying. None of it mattered. Except him.

He was the only reason I didn't need to be sedated at the thought of leaving. If I could just find him as soon as I was out of here, then everything would work itself out.

"Do you have any questions?" Nurse Sunshine asked.

"No."

Only then did her smile falter a bit. "Are you sure? I know it's a lot to take in, so it's perfectly okay to ask questions."

"I said," I emphasized. "I didn't have any."

"Well," she said, finally losing some of her annoying bubble-gum peppiness. "If you're sure then. I'll just give this to the doctor to sign. It shouldn't be much longer now."

When I didn't reply, she slunk away like a dog with its tail between its legs after getting yelled at for piddling on the floor. I almost felt bad for being a little shitty. Almost, but not quite. I stared up at the ceiling, waiting, my emotions, as usual, all over the place. Finally, a new nurse poked her head in, but she didn't enter, like she was afraid. I'd obviously hurt the other one's feelings.

"Miss Yates, all your discharge paperwork is in order. I have a wheelchair out here whenever you're ready."

"I don't need a wheelchair." I may not be quite ready to go, but since I was leaving it sure as hell wasn't gonna happen by any means except my own two feet.

"It's really hospital protocol that—"

"Fuck protocol," I snapped, rising from the bed and swinging my legs to the floor. "I don't give a shit about it. I'm not an invalid. I have two perfectly working appendages, and I plan on walking my happy ass out of this place. So, I'm free to go?"

"Y—Yes, you're free to go."

I rose from the bed, having already changed into the second-hand clothes the hospital chaplain had managed to find for me. I'd never been one for charity, but it was either this or get arrested for indecent exposure when the cops picked me up for being butt-ass naked. I didn't have many clothes, and the ones I did have were no doubt long gone. You left stuff at the shelter for too long, and you could kiss it goodbye.

Nurse Scaredy-cat stepped back, letting me pass by. It was pure stubbornness that I didn't apologize for my asshole behavior and beg them to let me stay a little bit longer. My entire body trembled as I held my head high and strode out of the hospital and onto the street, the small sheet of prescription paper in my hand.

It was a perfect day. The sun was shining and there wasn't a cloud in the beautiful blue sky. I tipped my head back, closed my eyes, and soaked up the heat of the rays hoping it warmed the chills that threatened to rack my body despite being the middle of summer. A honking horn ripped me from my daydream and thrust me right back into reality.

I glanced down at my skid-free yellow socks provided by the hospital. They were brightly colored and the first new piece of clothing I'd owned in over two years. The newness would wear off before I was ready for it to, just like everything did. No one truly appreciated new things. Not really. Anymore, everything was disposable. Don't like the car you drive? Trade it in for a different model. Tablet breaks? Buy a new one. Tear a hole in your jeans? Throw them away and get a new pair. Wear a hole in the big toe of your socks? Toss them and grab another three-pack.

With that, I bent down and pulled my new yellow socks off, wiggling my bare, unpolished toes. God, I couldn't even remember what nail polish looked like. I stuffed the two articles of clothing in the back pocket of the jeans someone no doubt had never even missed and started walking. I remained alert to my surroundings. I stayed on the main streets along the sidewalk, never venturing down any deserted side roads. The closer I got to where I was heading, the faster I moved, and soon I was nearly running.

Sweat dripped down the side of my face, between my

tits, and down my back by the time I reached my destination. My feet were also killing me, but I refused to put my socks back on. A little dirt and a small bit of blood from the piece of glass I'd stepped on was a small price to pay for keeping my only brand-new article of clothing clean.

"Excuse me," I said, my voice strong and even despite the terror coursing through me, to the man seated behind the plexiglass.

He glanced up at me with disinterest. "Can I help you?"

"I need to see Officer Oliver Garrison."

"Regarding?" he drawled, lazily.

"None of your business," I snapped, regretting it after he narrowed his eyes at me. "Sorry. It's a personal matter. An important personal matter."

The man heaved an annoyed sigh and picked up the phone. "Name?"

"Charity."

His brows raised as though waiting for a last name, but that was all he was getting. He rolled his eyes. "Have a seat."

"Thank you, but I'll just stand here." I was too anxious to sit. The buzzing and the feeling of ants were biting me would only increase if I didn't walk around.

"Suit yourself." He shrugged. "Who knows how long it'll take him to answer. He's probably out somewhere."

I'd stand here for as long as it took. I didn't care.

"Hey, it's McCrary. If Garrison is around, can you let him know that Charity is here to see him?"

Pause.

"No idea. She didn't say. Said it was a personal matter."

Another pause.

"Thanks." He hung up the phone and turned his gaze back to me. "They'll pass on the message."

I nodded, and began to pace, my bare feet slapping against the cool tiled floor. Person after person came through the lobby area of the police station, none of them Oliver. I jumped out of the way of a cop pulling a hand-cuffed man by the arm before they disappeared through a doorway and into the abyss of whatever lay past it. The constant din of conversation was making me twitchy and nervous.

"Charity?"

I spun at my name and nearly lost my balance but caught myself before taking a header. In the same doorway stood the man I'd come to see. His tattooed arms displayed bright blues, greens, reds, and yellows. He moved across the room, and his emerald green eyes darted around the lobby before landing back on me when only a few feet separated us.

"What are you doing here?" he asked, confusion evident. He glanced down at my bare feet. "Where are your shoes?"

"You're the only person I trust. The only person that makes me feel safe after everything they did to me. I'm scared, and I don't have anywhere to go." My voice broke, but I swallowed back the strangled sound. "I need your help. Please, Oliver."

Thank you so much for reading **BULLET PROOF**! I hope you enjoyed it. If so, I'd greatly appreciate a review on the platform of your choice. Reviews are so important!

Who doesn't love a wedding? Ines and Brody finally tie the knot. Be sure to check out their Christmas wedding in FOR ALWAYS!

Can Oliver change his ways? Who exactly is Charity? Find out in POINT BLANK Coming March 2021 Preorder your copy today!

Have you started the Love Undercover series yet? Be sure to check out IN TOO DEEP. Turn the page for a preview.

IN TOO DEEP

"Kill him."

Those two, single-syllable words played on repeat like a litany in my ears. They were accompanied by a multitude of emotions.

Horror.

Guilt.

Satisfaction.

It's the last one that made me the most nervous.

I tried to pinpoint the exact moment things changed. The moment *I* changed. Was it the first time I took a hit of blow and loved the rush it provided? The time I sat on a piss-scented couch with a gun in my face, its hammer drawn back as incentive, while I "sampled" the latest stash of a new-to-me dealer who didn't quite trust me? Or maybe it was when I realized that sometimes, in order to make things happen, you had to get your hands dirty. I was on my own. No cavalry was coming to my rescue. I did what I had to to survive, even if I hated myself most of the time.

The drugs.

The killing.

They were all a part of the man I'd become over the last five years in order to bring an entire organization crumbling to the ground. It was my life's mission. My obsession, in fact.

Like an out of body experience, I watched my hand remove the gun from its shoulder holster and point it at the bleeding man begging for his life on his knees in front of me.

"Please, don't do this. I told you where the money was. Please, I have a wife, a daught—"

Closing off my emotions, I squeezed the trigger. The bullet entered his brain, cutting his words off mid-sentence. The dead man collapsed onto the cement floor of the abandoned warehouse near Chicago's Lake Michigan, blood pooling next to his head.

Miguel Álvarez, the man who'd given the death order, spat in the direction of the body. "Let that be another lesson to those who steal from me."

He clapped me on the shoulder on his way to the black sedan parked just inside the warehouse doors. "Tomás, my friend, welcome to the family."

I remained there, unmoving, while I watched two men begin to wrap up the body for disposal. It would be weighed down and dumped in the waters of the Michigan, hopefully to never be found again. My expression remained impassive.

"You will come to the house, *sí*?" The voice called from behind my back. Forcing my eyes from the scene in front of me, I turned to face Miguel.

"Yes, sir, I'll be there soon. I have some quick business

to take care of first." I didn't flinch at his assessing stare. After a moment he nodded.

"Don't be long, Tomás." The warning tone was clear. "I want to introduce you to my nephew, Alejandro."

He disappeared inside the car, closing the door behind him. The Mercedes pulled away, and I continued to watch it until the tail lights disappeared. Leaving the cleanup crew to their task, I exited the stifling heat of the warehouse before jumping on my fully restored 1984 cherry red Harley Softail. I started her up, slammed my heel against the kickstand, and took off in the opposite direction Miguel had gone. Fifteen minutes later, I entered the Grant Park North parking garage and drove around until I reached the fourth level. I spotted an empty parking space next to a blue Honda. The passenger window of the Honda lowered at the same time I cut the engine.

"I'm in." I spoke to the shadowy figure of my handler sitting in the driver's seat without turning my head in her direction.

"What did you do?"

I gave a self-deprecating laugh. "What I had to, Landon."

There was a long pause. She finally replied with a voice full of understanding. "I see. Well, we both knew going in that something like this might happen. It's unfortunate, but it needed to be done. You'll be in touch soon, then?"

"Yes. I'll let you know when the next deal is going down."

Without another word, I cranked up the bike and took off. I drove down Michigan Avenue, burying my emotions. I'd been with the Drug Enforcement Administration for eight years. I was en route to the home of the man in charge of the second largest Mexican cartel in the United States. No longer was I Brody Thomas, D.E.A. agent. I was Tomás González, full-fledged member of the Juárez Cartel.

I ignored the guilt stabbing me deep in my gut. Diego Garcia may have been the first man I'd been forced to kill, but if I was going to bring down the cartel, he most likely wouldn't be my last. Besides, any man who got his wife hooked on dope and then prostituted her out to his friends earned a special place in hell.

There were so many different scenarios in which all this would be over. Oftentimes, in my dreams, I eradicated every drug off the street and was hailed a hero. Other times, I had occasional nightmares of my cover being blown and Álvarez having me killed. It didn't matter. I'd signed up knowing the risks. But never, at any time, did I envision it would be a sexy Latina bombshell who would eventually bring my world crashing down around me.

Get IN TOO DEEP today at your favorite retailer.

Be sure to sign up for my newsletter and download your copy of A Birthday Spanking, set in the Doms of Club Eden world!

You'll also receive updates about what I'm working on, alerts for sales and new releases, and other stuff I don't share elsewhere!

ACKNOWLEDGMENTS

With every book comes a laundry list of all the people who helped me along the way. Bullet Proof is no different. You all deserve my eternal gratitude for every bit of encourage-ment, brainstorming, and critiquing you gave me. I could not have written this book without you.

Thank you to Julia Sykes and Autumn Jones Lake. You two keep me sane. You listen to me rant. Bitch. Moan and complain. You listen when I need to whine. When I'm feeling salty. You guys are the best, and I love you to pieces.

Thank you to my editor, Dayna Hart at Hart to Heart Edit-ing. The shit you put up with, like my complete and utter inability to meet a deadline, and it's always with a smile and a kind word of encouragement.

Thank you to my writing coach, Lauren Clarke at Creating

Ink. Your positivity and insight into craft has made me a better writer. Your critiques are invaluable.

Thank you to J.R. Mathis for reading the first 16K of hot garbage I sent you and offering some great critique on how to improve several scenes.

Thank you to Gabby Barocio for helping me with the Spanish translations in this book.

Thank you to Bianca Blythe. This book would not have been finished on time without you. For real. Those last four days of sprints helped propel me to the finish line, and I owe the completion of this book to you. I am forever in your debt.

Thank you to all my readers. The ones who support me book after book. You've stuck with me over the years, and I appreciate you more than I can say.

Doms of Club Eden
Forever (DoCE Prequel)
Submission
Desire
Redemption
Protect
Betrayal
My Christmas Dom
Absolution

Love Undercover Series
In Too Deep
Striking Distance
Atonement
Bullet Proof
For Always
Point Blank

Brooklyn Kings - Coming 2021
The Devil I Don't Know
The Enemy in My Bed
The Beast I Can't Tame

Other Books
Love Notes: A Dark Romance
SEALs in Love
Say Yes
Black Light: Possession
Saving Evie: A Brotherhood Protectors Novella

ABOUT THE AUTHOR

LK Shaw resides in South Carolina with her high mainte-
nance beagle mix dog, Miss P. An avid reader since childhood, she became hooked on historical romance novels in
high school. She now reads, and loves, all romance sub-
genres, with dark romance and romantic suspense being
her favorite. LK enjoys traveling and chocolate. Her books
feature hot alpha heroes and the strong women they love.

Want a FREE short story?

Be sure to sign up for her newsletter and download your
copy of A Birthday Spanking, set in the Doms of Club
Eden world!

http://bit.ly/LKShawNewsletter

Made in the USA
Columbia, SC
14 February 2021

32933846R00143